Hollywood Marine Vision

Asmar Muhammad

PAGE PUBLISHING, INC.
New York, NY

First originally published by Page Publishing, Inc. 2018

ISBN 978-1-64214-250-1 (Paperback)
ISBN 978-1-64214-251-8 (Digital)

Printed in the United States of America

In 1951 on an air force base called Travis, a Negro boy child was born to an airman, the first born to Richard Leon Brown. His mother was a pretty black woman who was seventeen years of age. Her name was Marilyn E. Crawford. Her family came to California from New Orleans. Thirty-three miles north of San Francisco, they lived in a small town named after General Vallejo. Near Vallejo is an island where the general kept his horses; it is called Mare Island today. The bay has hot days and cold nights with fog that rolls in from the Pacific Ocean.

In 1951, UN forces halted Red Drive in Korea, Amendment XXII of the Constitution limited presidents to two terms, the hydrogen bomb was tested, US Supreme Court upheld the rights to require signing of non-Communist affidavits by job applicants, Hearst (a flamboyant news tycoon) died at age eighty-eight, and at age seventy-seven, Winston Churchill returned to power in Britain. The president was Harry S. Truman, and vice president was Alben W. Barkley.

In sports, Michigan shut out California (14–0) in Rose Bowl, Lee Wallard won Indy 500 in Belanger Special (averaging 126 mph), Yankees beat Giants (4–3) in sixth game of World Series, Navy trounced Army (42–7) in annual football game, and Joe DiMaggio announced retirement from baseball.

In music, we have *Billy Budd* and *King and I*. Academy Award winners were the following: Vivien Leigh in *A Streetcar Named Desire* and Humphrey Bogart in *The African Queen*. It births Evonne Fay Goolagong, an Australian tennis champion.

Prices in the 1950s: postage stamp was $0.03, bread was (pound loaf) $0.16, milk (quart) was $0.23, gas (gallon) was $0.27, and car was $2,330. Minimum wage was $0.75. Median family income was $3,709.00.

The old Jim Crow laws were in effect in the south and the west to some degree. There were no black and white drinking fountains, but class and race played a major part in the 1950s. We stayed in base housing, which was all blacks. It was a project housing. My dad attended Vallejo High School and went to school with Dick Bass, a famous football star.

Dad's best friend was the Rev. Lee Armstrong. This was a major problem with my grandmother, who was a deeply devoted Catholic raised by nuns in the French quarters of New Orleans. My grandfather was the son of a famous jazz player whose name is listed in the New Orleans Hall of Fame. My grandfather's father is one of the names who started off jazz music. He came to California but hated it because they didn't like his flashy outfits. He used to cook red beans and rice on stage and drink wine while he played. In those days, blacks did not eat with white folks.

Grandma was a big-boned light-skinned woman, like the very strict nuns who would smack you with the ruler or make you sit in the corner of the room. She was mixed with Native American and French. She had long black hair. The naval years drew folks from New Orleans west in search for a better life after the war. Granddad worked for the church and drove truck and gave food to the poor blacks and others in town of Vallejo. He was known as Mr. C by all the kids at the high school. His house was high on top of a hill, Pecan Street.

My grandmother and he were deep in love, and she kept her home super clean. She cooked and cleaned. If we made a mess, she would beat the hell out of your backside, so we kids spent most of the time in the carport. She made the best gumbo this side of New Orleans, sometimes taking a week to make the dish at Christmas. Our family sits down with candles and love and with pictures of white Jesus in the living room, along with family photos everywhere.

My dad's family, led by Mrs. Jackson Brown, took care of me at times. She lived next to the Safeway store in the center of town. The base housing was small, and my parents were at odds most of the time. My dad was a fireman on post and began to abuse his pretty teenage wife.

I recall as a young child my mother cutting her feet with clippers. It was the first time I ever saw blood. I thought she was dying, and I remember crying without end. But later, this would be minor compared to the placing of a knife to my mother's neck while I sat helpless in a high chair. I didn't understand why any man could do that to my only love, my mother, who fed me from her breasts. I thought he was going to kill her.

I will never forget that day for as long as I live. Later, she would remarry. I didn't like him, but he paid the bills, and he was a role model. But in time, he would abuse her also. At times, I thought it was something I did, and at times, she made me feel bad about myself because I reminded her of my dad. As a child, I didn't understand why. It would take me years as a man to come up with a reasonable answer. And the same thing happened to me with my relationship with my wife. I abused her, but now, not to the point of trying to kill her, but abuse is abuse. As a young man, I had forgotten the lesson of pain shown at a young age.

Soon I had a brother and sister. I would care for them both. In the old days, they had cloth diapers, and I would shake the shit in the toilet. They were then washed and hung out to dry. Everyone had lines to hang their things. We used scrubbing boards and sunshine to dry. Women would even hang their private things on the lines, which was a great wonder as a male child. I would show my brother and sister how to wash dishes and do little things around the house. Since I was the oldest, it was my duty to teach them how to do homework and housework.

My sister, Romel, was a quick study, and later in life, her profession was teaching special education in the poor black areas of Sacramento. My brother was a bit slower, but being younger, he learned from my mistakes. He was a better student, but the code of the streets was that you had to fight, right or wrong, for the right to be number one in the pecking order. Romel would try to cook breakfast, but it just wouldn't turn out right, and Mom would make us eat it anyway, lumps and all. She didn't waste food! She almost never got spanking, but I got the most because I was the oldest and Mom thought I should know better. And sometimes we got our butts whipped just because Bob and I would get into some trouble. Grandma would pull our ears from the backyard to the front. We were like Robin Hood. We raided every fruit tree on the block, and back in those days, they were everywhere. We even ate the green fruit and got the runs. We stole Coke bottles from under porches and storage sheds for candy refunds. We used to hide in the trees and throw eggs at any white person who walked down the street. They never knew where the rocks came from; they had rows of trees everywhere.

We made real bows and arrows from trees and used real BB guns and played my first war games with all the kids in the hood.

Grade School

Vallejo is near the Napa Valley. The Napa valley is known the world over for some of the best wine in the world, perhaps as fine as any French brand. You see, more wine heads in Vallejo as a result of cheap wine everywhere. My uncle Richard would even make his own stock, red and white. Therefore, as kids, we would run away for some nut who had too much to drink. Many slept in alleys and scared us kids, just because they could. I think I became good at track because I needed the running skills. They never got me, too fast. On the first day of school, my mother walked me to school. It was not far from the projects. Mom took me there about a week. On the second week, things were different. She put my lunch money in my top shirt pocket. The money was for milk and graham crackers. I was walking alone when out from behind some trees, some older female students attacked me. My first ambush!

They beat me up and stole my lunch money, ripping my shirt and getting away with the loot. They showed no mercy. I didn't see women or girls as the weaker sex from that day forward; some of them could fight just as hard as guys. Even so, I never fought my sister; I knew it was my job to protect her.

Exceptional Classroom

In those days, thing were different. The police never took kids from homes. Parents had more control because the school and the whole town could beat your butt if you were wrong. And no one would call in the police. I was glad I went to public school, and the headmaster would take out the paddle for any class problems, but I hated going to the church on demand by Grandmother because the nuns were far worse. They had ten million ways to make you suffer. In those days, there was no such program as special education class, not even for the blind student or the retarded student. The teacher had her class full to the max!

I am surprised I learned anything. Maybe there were thirty different kinds of kids, and to make things worse, many kids were not allowed to go the next grade without learning all the lessons, so many kids (some almost teenagers) were kept back. I was held back a year, and I don't think I was too bad, but it was hard to focus with so many kids and so many things going on. One teacher had no time for us all. My math and English skill were poor. I tried to help my brother. I was a below-average student, but I guess it was okay because we were black kids, and no one really cared. And of course, there were fights, and if a white kid called you a nigger, you could beat his ass, and that was acceptable and normal. There were fights every day going and coming home from school. There was summer school for kids to get one last chance to go to the next level.

On weekends, Grandpa Joe would give us toys from St. Vincent de Paul truck route. We didn't care that they were old or used. We had more toys than most of our friends. So we would share. We had old baseball gear, with bats and balls, football shoes, cars, boats, dolls, electric trains, etc. My dear mother would try to buy us dress shoes for school, but that didn't work. We boys ran out of them very fast.

So she got boots, which lasted longer and helped with fights after school. The teacher was under so much pressure.

There were blind kids, retarded kids! One boy we called Tank Head because he had a huge head. At first, kids made fun of him, but once you got to know him, you kind of felt sorry for him. And the blind kids I helped get in their seats. And I wondered how they could understand small balls written in their books and on the bathroom and hallways walls.

My mother made us write book reports in the hot summer days. We had to read all the classic books, *Huck Finn, Sinbad the Sailor, Tale of Two Cities*. She just wanted our heads in all kinds of books, books to read, even comic books, which was up to my liking. *Batman and Robin*, my new role models, we collected them and sold them, a dime each for brand-new copies. With a new book, with pictures and words and action, all you needed were some sunflowers seeds and some Red Vines, and your day is set. Imagination is about to take off to who-knows-where. A lot more interesting than *Huck Finn*. Dream about the future and visit the past. There are no limits to the imagination. A fresh mind that is open for anything. Red Vines and seeds. Life is good.

Superman and Batman were the best. I loved the Batman because he had no powers like Superman. He used martial arts and trained his body and mind, and his money was a tool to reach his goals. Superman was the man of steel, and he could fly. He showed us the future in the sixties with drones, robots, and people with different hair colors—blue, green, and gold. I found out I wasn't Superman when I shot a handmade nail gun, and it backfired and sent a nail in the middle of my forehead, which my loving mother pulled out. I think that opened up my third eye. On the sellevision, there were tons of cowboys and Western Indians, like Gun Smoke, Rifleman, and Rin Tin Tin. I love the brave culture of the native peoples. No blacks on the sellevision. Amos and Andy were playing fools. I love Nat King Cole and Sammy Davis Jr. Sammy was a real quick gun art-ist in real life with guest-starring roles. I remember Jackie Robinson at bat. White people booed him for about ten minutes, saying, "We are going to kill you nigger." And you could hear it loud on the air waves. I was thinking, "What had he done to get such treatment?" Later I saw the great Willie Mays find a fly ball and make the play behind his back, and threw the ball from center field to get a player out at home plate. Wow! Never seen anything like that before.

Sellevision had some great shows in the past like *The Outer Limits*, *Hitchcock Presents*, *The Man from U.N.C.L.E.*, and all movies were shown free on public TV. All sports were free. The priest would post a list of the movies that the church folk could see and a list of movies that the church banned. It was all a form of mind control. The priest represented God's view on earth, but most drank wine and cussed like my future drill instructors. My dear grandmother would wash out our mouths with soap if we used the damned words. The white man has not come to the impact of the terms and words that make you feel less than human . . . a bad period being born black. ADD and PTSD had not been coined. No police broke up families for bad behavior. Spanking were given by everyone to kids, by parents, grandparents, nuns, headmasters, and folks down the street you didn't even know. One day at the park, I went under a wire fence, and a white man shot me with rock salt for being on his land. That scared the hell out of me. I though he was going to kill us.

One of America's top actors at that time lived in Vallejo, Raymond Burr. He was the star of a hit TV show called *Perry Mason*, a courtroom drama. All of America never knew he was gay. He even had a wife. In court, he always won his cases. Janice would become a lawyer, and I think Raymond had some impact. He was very cool under pressure and found ways to bring justice. The real facts were the trick in every case. The first actor I loved and hated at the same time was the actor who played Superman in the TV show. I know now that acting is not real, but as a kid, to hear that the man who played Superman had killed himself with a gun was unbelievable! A real actor who could not get any other roles in Hollywood, but the man of steel. As a black actor, it's hard to get any kind of role, so I think that white man flying around just coped out. He really upset me and pissed me off. Damn you, Superman! I bet he never knew of all the kids like me who jumped off roofs and died on some wire trying to be like you.

I realized how human I was when I stuck a pole down a wasp nest and the yellow-and-black wasp attacked my entire body. It seemed like hundreds of them covering my eyes and falling down only to be hit again and again. Stings made my whole face blow up like Tank Head, the boy kids made fun of, and Mother nursed me back to normal! Learn to respect the home of insects. A mother cat would dig deep claws in my body to protect her kittens.

Dumb kid, I ate pussy for the first time at six because of a teen-ager who watched us while my parents went out. I didn't know what the heck I was doing, but the payment of a tall glass of Strawberry Quik was a good motivation. I was the sellevision quick master in pussy eating in no time flat. There I remember a funny lady on TV saying, "There is nothing an old man could do for her but bring her a young man." Later in life, my pussy-eating skills were a way to take and keep a woman, sometimes from other women. I think back in the day, most men, black men, didn't eat pussy. Do I get a head start or what?

Photographic Memory

A person capable with accurate and lasting impressions has photographic memory. By 1965 the worst day of my life had passed. The president of the United States was laid to rest and was covered on every channel on sellevision. I began to wonder what kind of people lived in the world and what evil really was.

Cassius Marcellus Clay (a.k.a. Muhammad Ali) had won the gold medal in 1960 and was soon to fly to England to fight Henry Cooper. I never could imagine that I would ever leave America to see and to walk on British soil on the other side of the earth—the United Kingdom, the land of our former slave masters.

Each day had been replaced by a new man in my mother's life. Mom had remarried Staff Sergeant Sylvester Parker. And we had to accept the fact that my father was no longer in the picture, and my sister Cerice was the result of that union. Being the oldest, I tried to buck the outsider male, but to his credit, he had a smart mind. He didn't forget anything. He fixed his own cars with the right tools.

He kept the house squared away and remembered every detail of any event that occurred. The rebels were soon under control by the empire. The rebels being myself and my brother Bob.

UCMJ 89

Disrespect toward the superior commissioned officer. Any Marine who behaves with disrespect toward his superior commissioned officer shall be punished as his commanding officer or a court martial may direct.

As a young lad, this was my induction into the life of service to the United States military way of life. He beat our butts. He made us clean the entire house. Any taken task he gave was to be followed to the letter. He showed us how to use tools the correct way. We cleaned and pressed our outer wear. We built fish tanks. We used electric table saws. We used tape measures and levels, made our beds in the correct form, called him sir, and no longer used foul or bad words in his watch. Our and his shoes were spit-shined. Everything had a place, and every tool had a location. If these tasks were not done correct, we would get a beating. Playtime was over. The road to manhood was going to be hard but fair in his eyes. Soon he got orders to ship out to a small air force base in England. This move would change my entire life. A new dad and a new place both emitted the unknown.

For Your Eyes Only (Part 1)

Ian Fleming was read by this lad some time before we landed in the UK. I read all of his books. I'm sure I have read all twelve books before I was fifteen. Most folks don't know that the spy character James Bond was based on Mr. Fleming's service in the British Marines as a naval commander during the Second World War. Pinewood Studios is where the movie takes place. It's famous for *007, Superman, Star Wars*, etc. I met the first James Bond, played by Sean Connery, at the American Films Award (AFI) at the Cinerama Dome in Hollywood (2013).

Never in my wildest dreams would I go to United Kingdom. I would represent my country, America, like Muhammad Ali represented his, and we were both disrespected by white people when we returned home to Jim Crow laws and hatred for our people. Like brothers, he and I never returned that hate. It just wasn't our way of heart. But he was brave to stand up and not care about the money or fame. I have met many so-called movie stars and important persons (VIPs), but he stands alone. I remember praying with him, and the leader of the group said, "God is great and the Lord of all, and he is the maker of us all, no matter what our position is in life. To him we give praise and to him we all return."

Road Trip

In the sixties, there was only one car on the road with four spark plugs, and that was a VW bug. All other cars had V8s. Even the six-cylinder cars had not been made for the road yet. Now the only Honda I have was a lawn grass cutter. The VW had four bolts holding the motor; it was air-cooled and could be removed and replaced in about four hours. It had two six-volt batteries under the seat and a flapper on each side. It also had a switch to turn on when the car was empty. That gave you an extra gallon of gas.

Going south from Vallejo, about thirty-three miles is San Francisco. We left early in the morning; it only takes about seven hours' drive to Los Angeles. I remember taking field trips to the Bay City. As kids, we went to the famous pier to see the boats and eat the fresh seafood and to Chinatown, the largest population in America. Bruce Lee had a gym there and taught kung fu after he left Seattle. Many in that town have no need to learn English. The San Francisco museum is where I saw the oldest cheese in the world; it's dark black. It is displayed in a glass cage.

The San Francisco Zoo has lots of animals. The ones I remember were the monkey who threw their shit at the tourist. And we also went to the best wax museum in the United States at that time. I had big funny smiles at the fun house. It had crazy mirrors and bending floors. We were leaving all this behind and our family. The tall wind turbines had not been placed in the hills of Oakland yet; it was naked with grassy rolling mountains and hills. As you drive down toward Los Angeles, you see miles and miles of rich farmland. There were all kinds of fruits and nuts and vegetables, dates, wine rows, olives as far as you could see. They were picked by Mexican laborers who worked all day in the hot sun, picking and planting everywhere. About halfway, you begin to see large ranches of horses and cattle. Thousands in a herd. You could smell them before you saw the landscape filled with prime beef.

Gas was about $0.36 a gallon in those days. And when you pull up for gas, a man would run up to your car. He would check your oil and transmission with his rag, fill your tires to the correct air pressure, pump your gas, and wash your windows for free. You may tip him a quarter, and he was happy. There was no self-service in those days. The station did everything.

This was a good way to service your tires if needed, or change your belts, hoses, etc. There was a pay phone. With a dime, you could call localities with operator. The speed limit was 70 mph. And tickets for speeding had to be paid in the local town. A generator light came on if the car needed charging. The starter motor was very heavy, about thirty pounds. Crooks would try to steal your gas at night with an Oklahoma credit card, which was a cut-off lawn hose put in the tank. When sucked on, the pressure would drain any and all the gas in the tank. There was no locking gas caps. Plus the gas had lead in it. Cars still had carburetors with fuel and air mixture screws at the base. Like the old motorcycles, you can adjust the points with a flathead screwdriver and a business card for a gauge.

There were two-lane highway and a large channel of water running north and south, all the way down the west coast. Finally, you reached the grapevine, a little city at the base of a large mountain, going five thousand feet above sea level toward the stars if your car didn't overheat. Over the mountain pass, another seventy miles past Pyramid Lake, you would reach the second largest city in the United States, Los Angeles.

There were church missions up and down California. This was because in the old days, a horse ride was used between missions. Most were near a fort in case you were attacked by Indians. After the gold rush, Sacramento became the capital, which still has a mission and a fort.

We move on. We see New Mexico, then Amarillo, Texas. Not far from Amarillo is Lubbock, a small place famous for a rock-and-roll group, Buddy Holly and the Crickets. Buddy was killed in an airplane crash. At night, you can hear lots of crickets. The males of many species produce a shrill and chirping sound by rubbing the front wings together.

In Amarillo, they had gas wars. It was as low as $0.15 a gallon. A beef steak was about $0.50 cents. I like mine well done. I saw blood on most of the white folks' meat. I could not eat the whole thing; it was just too big. Now, Oklahoma. I loved the movie, and the music was outstanding too. I love to sing the opening song. People white and black had a southern drawl. Texas is a very flat state, and on that day, it was sunny, then it began to rain with the sun out, then rain turned into a hailstorm and destroyed some roofs in homes and convertible cars.

We could see the flashes of lightning fire the whole sky, and then the boom of powerful thunder. This is the God's voice speaking to us small kids. I feared it!

The Right Place at the Right Time

One of the best days of my life was the time I saved two kids from harm. In the Marines, I saved the day when smoke from a fag had lit a mattress from someone smoking in bed. I jumped out a second-floor window and ran down the street and pulled the fire alarm. No thanks given! Okay! But many years later, I saw two kids about three years old, brother and sister, running down an alley. It was the same alley used in the movie *Training Day*, but this was no movie. I was going to unlock the carport when I saw these two babies running full speed past me, I can't run fast, but I managed to stop them, and I asked, "Where is your mother?" They didn't know, so I said, "Let's go to your house!" And we walked a hundred yards back through this alley where fools race their cars and could care less about the folks that live there. I found their house and told the older sister what happened, the gate being opened by the older brother. I felt really good knowing I saved the kids from harm. It felt really better than any movie I was in or any money I could have gotten. Thank you, God, for putting me in the right place at the right time!

Veterans Hospitals

I have never liked VA hospitals with rude nurses and crazy people in waiting rooms. Some nurses leave needles in your arms forever, it seems like. They give you unseasoned food; you might as well eat cardboard. I never liked Jell-O. I worked at their factory and saw how it is made. It's lemon peels and orange peels processed; they add favors. The heat in your belly makes it swell up and trick your mind to think the belly is full! But the doctors are outstanding. Most come from UCLA and have gained my trust many times after many years of vehicles running over your feet and laying down motorcycles to escape harm. This time at the veterans hospital was different. The doctors explained that my foot was deformed and they could correct it! Scott Boynton and Jonathan Thompson were top surgeons. I could tell by the nurses' faces, these two were real alpha males. "Thank you for your service," I said before it was lights out. The clock read 8:00 a.m.; my last meal was 02:00 a.m. At noon, I woke up without tubes in my nose. But before long, it pained hard and fast. I wasn't crying; it was more like moans. I felt . . . better. I saw a PTSD service dog who sensed my pain begin to yelp.

A friend and fellow actor Tina Clark picked me up and took me the long route home using her maps. I made it upstairs without passing out. Once inside, water was all I drink. And then as I lay on my bed, something happened. I don't know if it was the drugs or a *vision*. I talked to the master teacher Buddha. He came in a dream. He told me to rest and keep quiet. No movies, no music, no talking on the phone calls. I had a high fever, and my mouth was dry like sandpaper. Buddha told me I would heal faster sitting still, not moving at all. For three days, my body had sharp pains, but my mind was at complete peace. I sat calmly and cleared my mind. My body was weak, but my mind was supercharged. It became clear.

Allons-y: Burning Daylight

In Little Rock, Arkansas, we landed at Sergeant S. Parker's home, where his brother and mother greeted us. She lived in the poor black side of town in a warm old house with a front porch. It was the first time in my life seeing a lightning bug or firefly. The used bioluminescence during twilight to attract mates. All the kids shoot watermelon seeds at them as they danced in the air. The next morning, his mother fed the whole crew with eggs and bacon, and homemade ginger bread, the best I have ever had to this day! It rained hard and fast. It poured so hard it seemed it was coming down sideways. Sly's brother rushed outside to bring the chickens in the house. We all laughed as Clay did what he was told. At first light, Sergeant S. Parker hugged and kissed his mother, and we packed the car and soon were reading plated cars bearing Tennessee State. I remember seeing green high mountain roads that if you look over the side too long, you would have fear of falling off. You could hear horns boom as trucks with heavy loads begin to down-shift five thousand feet in the mountain air.

Excusez Moi

Now we are almost to our final stop. The Pennsylvania Tupe pipe ride, and we will reach McGuire Air Force Base, New Jersey. Our family's cross-country trip would almost be over when out of the blue I saw it! After I saw it, I realized how much white people really hated Jews, brown, yellow, red, and black folks. I was only a kid, but the only person who could not read was my baby sister Cerice. After I understood what I read, I cried. It made an unforgettable scar on my soul—a scar that never healed, but then I understood what Jackie Robinson was dealing with going to the plate, with all foolish white fans calling him the N-word and saying they wanted to kill him. I saw horror face-to-face. When I saw it, I knew what a little Jewish girl named Anne Frank felt like. She was my sister that day, sitting in the front seat. She was my sister who I only read about in books. That day, she was alive, sitting next to me. North Carolina was no different than most states we travel through by car. They all had large billboards, and they had advertisements in public places or alongside highways, showing great places to eat, sleep, buy homes, gas stops, etc.

But this billboard in North Carolina was broadcasting evil for one and all to see. This little town bragged that their little one-horse town was the home of the Ku Klux Klan. Sergeant Parker never stopped for gas. There in fact he punched his big V8 and made sure his family made Virginia before nightfall.

We were not hanging around to see how many blacks lived there. One good thing for me I later learned was that not all whites had a black heart. This was a life lesson to see evil as evil. And the worst part is that billboard is being imputed in every brain on earth, scaring each and every one of us in super-seconds, fogging our brains from that clear beginning into the deepest mud.

We Land in the United Kingdom

Back in those days, they had airplanes made in Seattle, Washington. The 707 Boeing, is a mid-sized, long-range, narrow-body, four-engine jet airliner. Goodbye, America, my home sweet home. About ten hours later, we touched down at the Dublin Airport, and we stayed on the plane for a few minutes. It appears that the London fog, which the city is so famous for, had covered London's Heathrow Airport.

I saw with my own eyes what Ian Fleming had called *thrilling cities*. Sergeant S. Parker and his new family had landed in an ocean of white people; none had hatred in their eyes. It seemed that we were the only dark folks around for miles, and I could tell some had never seen blacks from America. They knew we were yanks by our gear and the speech. Most British people love America because together they worked to end the war. The first house we lived in had a large green-coated mole, open brick walls which blended with the grass. But it had steps that led into a dark room. This was a real bomb shelter. We used to play in it, but it was a real reminder of the bombs that fell from the sky. That space could hold up to ten people. I could sense at that age that war was wrong. I met people in England and the EU. The common people are wonderful; it's always the leaders who run amok!

On Her Majesty Secret Service

At the guest room in the hotel, the wooden floors were polished, with large tables and chairs, and desks with panels that folded down to write letters. There were large clocks that bonged on the hours; some made music and went back to work. We even had a fireplace to every room. The only thing it didn't have was the first question I asked the maid. I asked her, "Where is the bathroom?"

"What's a bathroom?" she asked, then said, "Oooh, you mean the WC?" Then she walked me down the hall to a wooden door, the sign WC on it.

"But what does WC mean?"

"It means water closet, Master Richard." She had just opened my young mind to this brave new world. My analytical skills sky-rocketed. I could see the very old and new in the same form. Romans built roads, straight made of cobblestones, houses with green plants that covered brick walls all the way to the roof. The men and women had suits made of 100 percent wool and hats. They greeted each other with words of positive feeling.

"Cheerios, old chap," or a simple "Good day" rolled of their lips, and that was who they are—honest and straightforward. They had slang words. For example, women or girls were called birds! Fags were no gay. When you lit up a fag, you were smoking a cigarette. Gays were called queer.

The rest of the family began to experience culture clash. Also, we were all sitting at a kitchen table with proper setting and every fork and spoon in a proper place. We ordered steak but sent it back to be recooked. This time, it was Mother who would be hit with culture clash. The maids were young; they may have been my mother's age. We were eating all fancy, and the maids poured wine. Our first night in England went well so far, but one maid said something to my stepdad that changed everything. She said in a normal voice, "What time should I knock you up in the morning?"

My mother sprang to her feet quicker than Muhammad Ali. "You are not knocking nothing with my husband." She was ready to throw down. Robert and I laughed but not too loud. Who would have thought these words have different meanings in different parts of the world? Our education had just begun. New things to learn. The metric system was in full effect. The British pound in those days was twenty US dollars. Drinking teas from around the world is what the British people do. At least seven times a day, they drink tea. It was a very refined place. Policemen had bully clubs. They are called bobbies and didn't carry firearms. We never needed them for our three-year tour. Islam was a respected worship. Africa would send the top minds here to learn and educate its people.

The Man with the Golden Typewriter (Part 1)

England, like America or any other place, had a dark side. Our family lived in only two places in England in our three-year tour. The first village was called Little Kingshill in the parish of Little Missenden, five miles west of Amersham and about two and a half miles south of the second city we stayed, Great Missenden. Little Kingshill is where we lived in a cottage with a bomb shelter. In the back was a large area for cows that ran all the way to the main road. Next to us was a family of four, and the mother was an English schoolteacher. About a year in, we moved into the largest house I will ever live in. The house was over a hundred years old made of solid brick, and I would bet my last dime she is still there today! This fine lady of a house is part of an affluent village, Great Missenden, with some two thousand residents in the Misbourne Valley in the Chiltern Hills in Buckinghamshire.

Missenden is derived from the Old English for "valley where marsh plants grow." Then the town has this doctor who has some dark-side dealings. Sir Francis Dashwood was a physician and also a senior member at the Hellfire Club. The Hellfire Club was for several exclusive clubs for high-society rakes established in Britain and Ireland in the eighteenth century. The is most commonly used to refer to Sir Francis Dashwood's Order of the Friars of St. Francis of Wycombe. Such clubs were rumored to be "person of quality" who wished to take part in socially perceived immoral acts, and the members were often involved in politics. Neither the activities nor membership is easy to ascertain, for the clubs were rumored to have distant ties to an elite society known as the Order of the Second Circle.

The Man with the Golden Gun

The Marine will be provided an M16A2 rifle. The Marine must point the rifle in a safe direction, must clear it correctly, must engage the safety mechanism, and must demonstrate how to carry it safely. Consider every weapon as loaded until you examine it and find it to be unloaded. Never trust your memory in this respect. An old saying among hunters is "An empty gun shoots the loudest." Never point a weapon at anyone that you do not intend to shoot or in a direction where an accidental discharge may do harm. Never fire a weapon until it has been inspected to ensure that nothing is in the bore. Firing a weapon with an obstruction in the bore may burst the barrel, resulting in serious injury to you or to your fellow Marines. Never grease or oil ammunition. Some foreign weapons are designed to use greased or oiled ammunition, but using such ammunition in your weapon will cause dangerously high pressure in the chamber and the barrel. Never place a cartridge in a hot chamber unless you intend to fire it immediately. Excessive heat may cause the cartridge to cook off. Do not allow your ammunition to be exposed to the direct rays of the sun for any length of time.

The Duties of a Prince with Regard to the Militia

A prince should have no other aim or thought nor take up any other thing for his study but war and its organization and discipline, for that is the only art that is necessary to one who commands. It is of such virtue that it is not only maintained by those who are born princes, but often it enables men of private fortune to attain that rank. And one sees, on the other hand, that when princes think more of luxury than of arms, they lose their state. The chief cause of the loss of states is the contempt of this art, and the way to acquire them is to be well versed in the same.

The Prince—Machiavelli (*Octopussy*)

Most civilians don't know what military life really means but coming from a brotherhood of warriors, and there will always be warriors! In this country, everyday men and women from all backgrounds, colors, creed, etc. swear before God and man that they will fight all foes from within and without America. All take the vow and promise without any force. There are no weapons being trained at your head. This vow is the most important mind-set for membership to enter the government's armed forces.

The recent police killing by ex-military personnel is by law a clear violation of the vow that these men took. And I would never call these men cowards. Rebels, they ace this leads to another problem. If lone wolves become packs and the government can't suppress them, soon law and order as we know it will be destroyed.

A small force of highly illicit trained warriors could cause major problems for any law enforcement group. This could cause a civil war. Most of the rebels will be young men who will fight back. They are not going to listen to a peaceful protest.

Diamonds Are Forever

The last time I saw the great Michael Jackson alive was at the largest funeral I ever attended, and that was the last time I saw Puffy Daddy Combs on stage. This super funeral had over two thousand people, and the man everyone came to honor was Johnnie L. Cochran Jr.

The best speaker that day was Geronimo Pratt, who later died in Tanzania. Mr. Pratt was the godfather of the late rapper Tupac Shakur (1998). Johnnie L. Cochran filed a federal law suit against the FBI and LAPD, accusing them of malicious prosecution and false imprisonment. Mr. Pratt spend twenty-seven years in jail and eight years in solitary confinement. In high school, he played quarterback, then joined the Army, serving two tours in Vietnam, earning two Purple Hearts and emerging a sergeant. Occupation was deputy minister of defense of the Southern California Chapter of the Black Panther Party. Elmer Gerard Pratt was also known as Geronimo Pratt or Geronimo Ji-Jaga Pratt.

Sergeant Garvin Long, USM6, twenty-nine years of age, was a decorated US Marine. He was also known as Cosmo Setepenra. He killed three police officers. Sergeant Long said it was a diabolical attack on the very fabric of society. "There is nothing more fundamentally important than law and order . . . That is not what justice looks like. It's not justice for Alton Sterling or anything else that has happened in this state or anywhere else. It's just pure unadulterated evil! The fact is you have to fight back against bullies. If for no other reason but to show you people. Bullies don't understand peaceful protest. They don't understand talking, only acting and fighting back."

Micah Xavier Johnson, twenty-five years of age, Afghanistan Campaign Medal with campaign star, Army Achievement Medal, Global War on Terrorism Service Medal, Armed Forces Reserve Medal. In July 7, 2016, in Dallas, Texas, Johnson killed five police officers and injuring nine others. Also, two civilians were wounded.

He stated he wanted to kill white people, especially white police officers. Target were white police officers in Dallas. Weapons were semiautomatic rifle and handgun. Sergeant Micah X. Johnson shot over two hundred rounds.

Charles Whitman, twenty-five years old, was one of the saddest Marine Corps story ever told. The Corps trained him to kill, and he took it to the limit. He earned a Good Conduct Medal and will be remembered as the Texas Tower Sniper. He was white. His occupation was engineering student. His targets were family, students, teachers, and police.

Weapons:

- Remington 700 ADL (6 mm)
- Universal M1 carbine
- Remington model 141 (.35 caliber)
- Sears model 19 (.357 Magnum)
- Sears model 60 semiautomatic shotgun (12 gauge)
- S&W19 (357 Magnum)
- Luger PO 8 (9 mm)
- Galesi-Brescia (25 ACP)
- Knife

All weapons were purchased that day (August 1, 1966). He shot forty-nine people within ninety minutes. Fourteen people died, and he also killed his wife and mother. "The greatest obstacle to discovery is not ignorance it is the illusion of knowledge" (Daniel J. Boorstin).

Back in the day, I was reading a paper called *Muhammad Speaks*. Now it is called the *Final Call*. "The State of Emergency" is the headline now. Back then, it was the "Fall of America." I was always interested in newspaper because when I lived in Seattle, I worked for a newspaper called the *Facts Newspaper*; it was the largest black-owned paper in the great northwest. In college, my minor was media, so I would take photos around Seattle and the editor, Mr. Fitzgerald Beaver. "The facts are reality" was on every newspaper heading at the Evergreen State College. One speaker was above all in terms of black Americans. His words are still important to my mind-set.

Every newspaper, white or black, knew his hard work and his exercise in intelligence. I never met Muhammad's Malcolm X, but that day I met the next best thing in a man called Stokely Carmichael (a.k.a. Kwame Ture). His new book, *Black Power: the Politics of Liberation*, was in every black student union member's hands. He came in a black car with bodyguards and two FBI cars tailing him. He talked how whites need to reform their communities to deal with stealing everything in the world and racism that exist.

He made a female student who was a so-called Jew crying madly, because he said all blacks must support the Palestine people against the oppression of the Jewish state of Israel. He was so direct and outspoken without any reserve. Later he was set up by Edgar Hoover COINTELPRO program. The head of the FBI tried to say he was a CIA agent. He was dispelled from the SNCC and the Black Panthers Party. Stokely Carmichael said that his cancer was given to me by forces of America's imperialism and others who conspired with them. He claimed that the FBI had infected him with cancer in an assassination attempt. He died at the age of fifty-seven. Rest in peace.

"If aliens call, we should be wary of answering!" Stephen Hawking is convinced that humans are not the only intelligent life in the universe. He also stated that if another form of life came here, it may be like the white man coming to do what white people did to the Native American people. Another man of science states not only is science corrosive to religion; religion is corrosive to science. It teaches people to be satisfied with trivialities, supernatural non-explanations, and blinds them to the wonderful real explanations that we have with our grasp. It teaches them to accept authority revelation and faith instead of always insisting on evidence. "When one person suffers from a delusion it is called insanity. When many people suffer from a delusion it's called religion" (Richard Dawkins).

Every time a black is murdered by a white cop, you see they always call on black preachers to cry for peace and calm the mob down. Stokely understood that the white man religions are really white power structures and the white man's god is money. Look at history. Did whites kill the native peoples and destroy their gods? For the record, did white people kidnap blacks and make them slaves?

Did whites use a bomb that killed thousands of yellow people? So one has to wonder and question, When is the god you pray for ever going to do anything to bring you justice in your life? Does God really exist?

Balls to the Wall?

(January 16, 1975, San Diego, day 1, USMC. Sunny day, seventy degrees, 07:00 a.m. A large green bus passes the MP at the front of the base. This is the Marine Corps Recruit Depot. About forty men are sitting side by side, talking and having a good time. Then the bus passes some Quonset Huts. To the center is a gigantic parade ground, and then in front and center is the recruit barracks. The bus makes an emergency brake, throwing heads forward. The door opens, and a black man wearing all green rushes inside the bus, screaming at the top of his lungs. Sergeant Clay was African-American, five-eleven with a chest full of ribbons and medals.)

STAFF SERGEANT CLAY: Get the fuck off the bus now, ladies, now. You maggots, move your feet and hit the deck and don't say a fucking word. Move, move, move, you broke-dick dogs.

(All the men fall from the bus are in some mass confusion. There are footsteps painted on the sidewall.)

STAFF SERGEANT CLAY: You girls smell like fresh fish. Stand at attention and don't say a fucking word.

(To our front was a big red sign, and it read: "To be a Marine, you have to believe in yourself, your fellow Marine, your corps, your country, your god. Semper fidelis.")

STAFF SERGEANT CLAY: Now listen up, you maggots. From now on, I'm going to be your mother, father, and when I give you an order, you better follow it to the letter, or there will be hell to pay! Do you understand?

MEN: Sir, yes, sir!

STAFF SERGEANT CLAY: If you bitches want to talk, you must first request permission to speak! Do you ladies understand that?

MEN: Sir, yes, sir!

STAFF SERGEANT CLAY: I can't hear you, girls. Act like you have a pair!

MEN *(all yelling)*: Sir, yes, sir.

(Staff Sergeant Clay sees me from the corner of his eyes; he sees me laughing to myself. Staff Sergeant Clay sees me from the right side.)

STAFF SERGEANT CLAY: Hey, you funny man, get over here front and center.

(I run over to his location.)

STAFF SERGEANT CLAY: What's your name, Private?

Me: I am Private Brown, sir.

STAFF SERGEANT CLAY: Do I look funny to you?

Me: No, sir!

SERGEANT CLAY: Then why are you eyeballing me? Down on your face and give me twenty-five pushups, and the rest of you ladies can follow his lead. Down, up, one, down, up, two, down, up, three . . . This time on the way down. I want you to say "Loyalty, sir!" and on the way up say "Discipline, sir!"

(Sergeant McFadyen, the drill instructor, is white male about thirty-seven years old, hard nose, no-nonsense kind of guy.)

DI MCFADYEN: Okay, ladies. I want you all to get ready for the big prom dance, but first we have to stop at the base barber so you can get dolled up. All haircuts are on me! And when you're done, you'll look like grasshopper on kung fu.

DI LODGE: For all you Jesus freaks and hippies, we are going. You are going to look like men in this man's Marine Corps.

STAFF SERGEANT CLAY: Platoon 1012, after you get haircuts, you will be given government-issued gear. Report to the chow hall. Dismissed!

(A long line waits to sit in two chairs with clipper set to the lowest level. Private Jordan is a white male about twenty-one years old long hair down to his neck.)

PRIVATE JORDAN: I didn't sign up for all of this! *(He began to cry silently.)* Why me?

(The barber cuts his long hair down until you could see his white scalp. His hair stacked up high from the floor to the top of his shoes. All the men were given a "high and tight" cut skull!)

Processing and Indoctrination

PRIVATE BRAWN: I remember protesting the war in high school. I was against the war even before Pitt's death. The good die young.

STAFF SERGEANT CLAY: This is government property. You will mark your name on all things that are given to you. You will secure all things in their proper locations. We will teach you essential subjects for you to become Marines.

PRIVATE HOLIDAY: Boy, we sure are getting a lot of shit . . . suits, coats.

PRIVATE BROWN: That wool coat alone is about $500 bucks on the streets!

STAFF SERGEANT CLAY: Boy, that's your problem. You are not on the streets no more. Jody is fucking your girlfriend, and now your ass belongs to me!

DI MCFADYEN: You ladies grab your trash and head back to the barracks, ASAP, now move!

The Barracks

(*The barracks was a large room, three hundred-by-fifty feet. There were rows of bunk beds, maybe thirty on each side, one small office for Staff Sergeant Clay, and a large restroom (head), with about ten stalls with toilets. At the foot of each bed was a large box to keep your personal belongings.*)

PRIVATE JORDAN: I am getting out of this shithole first chance I get! Fuck this place.

PRIVATE SHERMAN (*a white male from the south*): I think there are only two ways out the main gate, which ain't smart. There is a woman marine (WM) and has a big gun locked and loaded.

PRIVATE RODRIGUES (*Mexican American from New Mexico*): Or, you could try the freeway fence at night. Good luck with that one, mack!

Squid Bay Attention

(*All the men stood and saluted as Staff Sergeant Clay entered the room.*)
STAFF SERGEANT CLAY: Okay! I want every swinging dick in formation in sixty seconds, and we can head to the chow hall.

(Sergeant Major Crawford took the rear to make sure we all march together to his beat.)

Chow Hall

(*When we got to the chow hall, we all were told to take off our hats (covers). It also was a large room with metal tables long enough to seat forty men on each side. I was very interested because this is what I signed up for, my 3311. In front of the table were large glass squeeze guards to protect the metal trays with different foods. Night owls are what cooks are called!*)

SERGEANT MAJOR CRAWFORD: You got seventeen minutes to eat your chow and don't talk.

(*Lunch items were one-fourth-pound deluxe hamburger, one-fourth-pound deluxe cheeseburger, black bean burgers, veggie burger, grilled chicken, chicken filets, and French fries. The men dug in. It was the first good thing that happen to them all day. It wasn't home cooking, but it was that bad.*)

SERGEANT MAJOR CRAWFORD: In order to have a war, you need the three *B*s—Band-Aids to heal the troops, bullets, and beans.

(*We ran everywhere we when, so we ran back to the barracks.*)

Inside Barracks

STAFF SERGEANT CLAY: It's getting dark soon, and soon they will be playing taps at 22:00 hours, so until then let's have a PT party. The Marines want you to be strong and fit. So all you ladies, drop on your faces and give me twenty. Down, up, one, down up, two, down, up, three.

PRIVATE WALLSKI: I can't take no more!

STAFF SERGEANT CLAY: Eye, eye, which eye are you talking about? The left eye or the right eye, Private Ski?

PRIVATE WALLSKI: Request permission to stop, sir.

STAFF SERGEANT CLAY: Hell no, I know you are a fuck-up with a name like Ski on the ass end of it! All the rest of you ladies can help Ski out. Down, up, one, down, up two, down, up, three. (*Taps finally play, and we lie in our racks tired.*)

(*At 04:00 hours on day 2, the lights come up full power. The drill instructor runs in the middle of the barracks, takes a trash can and throws it in the middle of the air until it hits the deck with a low boom.* Blam!)

STAFF SERGEANT CLAY: Reveille, reveille, reveille, rise and shine, ladies! Get the fuck out the racks now and stand at attention. Get up, Private, and stand at attention in front of your bunk.

(*The men can't believe that the nightmare is real and this is not a bad dream. Some get to their feet slowly and in a mass confusion.*)

SERGEANT CLAY: Get on your feet. Get out of the fucking rack now. Hurry the fuck up.

ALL: Sir, yes, sir!

SSGT CLAY: We are going to do a three-mile run. And I want every swinging dick going all out. Am I clear on that?

ALL: Sir, yes, sir!

STAFF SERGEANT CLAY: I didn't hear you. Act like you got a pair!

ALL: Sir, yes, sir.

STAFF SERGEANT CLAY: You are going to be running from sunrise to sunset. I am going to run your dicks in the dirt. You maggots get your PT gear on and meet me outside in five minutes. Move, ladies.

(*Many of the troops started to fail to the hot dry dirt. I was lucky my track coach never lost a track meet, prepared us for this kind of training. I needed water badly, but I knew even at the age of twenty-three I could run a three-mile under eighteen minutes. My track coach named me Mr. PE the last year of high school. Many of the privates that day fell and got motivated by the drill instructor yelling and screaming them to finish. I moved forward.*)

TROOPS: If I die on the Russian front, bury me with a Russian cunt.

Left, right, left . . . left, right, left.

(*My ears were ringing from the sounds of airplane engines firing to lift off from the blacktop. It was so loud you could not hear your own heartbeat as your lungs cried for more air. My track coach was named Coach Gilbert. He never lost a track meet in the fifteen years he stayed at Highland High School. It was the main school by the air force base, so he knew many of the students were military families. He used to call me Brownie. I didn't like the name at first, but over time, I got used to it. Coach Gilbert died one year because a car jack fell on top of him. That's one reason I never get under a car without a jackstand.*)

*****

Part 1: Individual General Military Subjects (IGMS)

Provides Marines the essential military knowledge in such areas as the Uniform Code of Military Justice: Marine Corps history, customs, and courtesies, and close-order drill.

Part 2: Individual Combat Skills Subjects (ICBT)

Provides Marines the individual training packages (job aids) to serve as practical tools for training individual combat skills to standard.

Introduction to Individual Training Packages (Job Aids)

A job aid is divided into four parts. The following is divided description of each part (figure 1).

Task describes what the Marine must be able to do in combat conditions, describe equipment assistance, locations to do environmental considerations, etc., necessary to perform the task.

Standards describe how well the behavior must be performed.

Performance steps provide a logical sequence for executing the task.

The colors ceremony. In the middle of the base is a gigantic parade ground. It is about two miles one side and one-fourth mile wide. Every day, at 08:00 hours, the whole base comes to the parade deck to raise the flag. It is called the morning colors ceremony. The largest flag you will ever see is raised up a huge pole. It seems like ten troops take their time to present colors. Behind the barracks is a training field and a long gate that is the backside of San Diego Airport. This is where our three-mile run began.

*****

SERGEANT GARCIA (*age thirty-four to forty, a short Mexican-American, leads calling cadence*): Left, left, left, right, left.

TROOPS: Left, left, left, right, left.

SERGEANT GARCIA: There is only one color in this man's core, and that color is green.

(*It's hot, about eighty-five to ninety degrees, and there are about four rows of troops. It's running forward. Sergeant Garcia is running backward with a cigarette burning in his mouth. The troops were singing and running in cadence.)*

TROOPS: Sergeant, Sergeant, can't you see this PT is killing me? Left, right, left . . . left, right, left.

TROOPS: Up the hill, down the hill, around the hill, through the hill. Yoorah!

TROOPS (*running and singing*): If I die on the Russian front, bury me with a Russian cunt, left, right, left, left, right, left.

(We all drank water, lots of it. I fell to my knees and smiled, knowing I had finished my first goal, sweat pouring down from my face. The drill instructors are on privates like stink on shit. Slowly we walked back in formation. We reached the barracks and began to head to the chow hall. We saw steel tables lined up for eating the first meal of the day. A large sign is placed overhead: "CORNED BEEF HASH, TURKEY SAUSAGE, PORK SAUSAGE, COUNTRY BACON FRUIT TOPPING, EGGS, PANCAKES, BELGIAN WAF-FLES, CHEESE OMELET HAM AND CHEESE OMELET, WESTERN OMELET, VEGGIE OMELET, HASH BROWNS, MIX FRUIT, TOAST.")

DRILL INSTRUCTOR: You have got fifteen minutes to eat your trash, no talking, period. If I see you moving your lips, you will be asked to get the fuck up!

The Surgeon General's Report

TROOPS: The surgeon general has determined that smoking may cause death. We don't care, we are an elite fighting force called the Marines.

DI: All those with smokes, light them up.

(*I began to inhale the smoke, and my mind floated away to my dream girl. She was the love of my life.*)

*****

I met her at a park. She was young, about twenty-two years old, light-skinned, mixed with black and white, and she was very sexy and wild. She smoked weed, and she had done some time in the joint, for drug sells.

I pulled her away from the other guys, and we went to KFC. We used to drive to Riverside to go the club Metro and dance the night away. She would let me grind her ass on the pool table to the song "Back That Ass Up." That was our song. And she always had her eyes for other women, and she didn't care if other people knew she liked women. She hated the police. I knew she would never call the police if things went bad between us. She was a proud Long Beach Crips. She was a free soul, good-hearted person, and didn't believe in getting married, and if she did, it would most likely be a woman. I gave her a hundred dollars for some great sex. She took me to the track, where I met all the pimps watching the girls turn dates and get paid. I was her man, and she taught me the game. Pimps would steal girls from other pimps, but they respected each other, and at the end of the year, they would crown the pimp who got the newest cars and the most girls on their team. I used to watch her back for vice and the po-po.

Our time off the clock was pool. She was very good at the game. Lady B hated white girls even if she was mixed with white blood.

She had lots of hair, and you could see the black bloodlines with her afro. She would charge the white men $300 and up for a date. And she loved to do drugs. She loved X and speed and finally crack, and with a can of 211 each day, she made her skyfall. She went to Reno for two years, and I missed her every day. Reno is a small town, with a million people. I found her within two days on the track, and we picked up where we left off. I paid her bills to the dealers and took her back to Los Angeles. She was my dream girl in 1999. She was a real wild child. We would go camping at the state park close to the Pacific Ocean, have great sex, and listen to the waves at night from our tent. She was my soulmate in this life. She was okay with having sex with me and another woman. It happened one Super Bowl weekend, and it made me feel like a black king with two black queens. She was the best.

Weapons to the Head

The first time I had a loaded gun placed to my head was after I finished my training at MCRD, and it all happen because some loser dope-ass marine was pissed off because I had on my uniform when I went to San Diego to the clubs and bars downtown. What a prick. Of course, I told him I won't do it again.

I never reported him to the corps, but the next day, I went to the PX and got a new .45 Colt. It was gold-plated, and it was stolen by another Marine. The second time was when a bitch from LAPD stopped me for no reason as I left the unemployment office in Hollywood. I was dressed to kill in a suit, minding my own business, when she stopped me crossing the street. She pulled her weapon and told me to sit down on the ground next to her car's exhaust pipe while the car is still running. She didn't give me a reason why she stopped me, and the car's hot pipe was burning the back of my neck. After she let me go, I went to make a report at the LAPD headquarters in Hollywood with no results, and no charges were ever filed against her. I'm not surprised the reports of killing unarmed black men are so high in LA. Thugs in uniform with no mild treatment for blacks or others who are not white. Under the uniform code of military justice, many of LAPD officers would be court-martialed and discharged. The laws of the State are a can of worms.

Return to the chow hall in a nick of time, with jumbo hot dogs, chili cheese dogs, French fries, onion rings, baked potato, coleslaw, fruit cups. My MOS was to be a cook for the corps and a baker, so all the cookies, cakes, pies to be made for thousands would be my job along with the rest of the food. One any given day I would cook for 1,500 troops, plus go to the rifle range and do my PT run of three miles, morning, noon, and night, from, 04:00 till 22:00 hours. I used to cook so much that food was in my skin, and taking a bath didn't always release the small shit on my body. The best day for cooking was the Marine Corps birthday with hundreds of cakes, pies, etc. And of course, they had the largest BBQ pit I have ever seen. It must have been four hundred feet long with cases of steak to be burned in the fire. You have to remember that in those days we didn't have machines to cut the potatoes. We have to do it all by hand. That would mean hundreds of boxes to prepare.

Back to Basic Training

(*We all return from chow. We all wear our uniforms with starched hats, belts, boots shined, emblems worn correctly, all directed by our DI, Staff Sergeant Clay, a veteran of Vietnam who saved men under fire in the war.*)

STAFF SERGEANT CLAY: Jones, Washington, Holiday, Waski, Brown, Smith, Carter Clark, Harris, Crawford, you all got mail call. Private Brown you got a large packet here, smells good like homemade cookies, I know you are going to share them with young fellow marines, are you? (*He then passes them out to all the troops but me.*)

PRIVATE BROWN: Sir, yes, sir! I tried not to show any reaction to him giving away my mother homemade cooking. But it did hurt.

SERGEANT MCFADYEN: Private Brown, do you have any Kinfork that serve this country soldier?

PRIVATE BROWN: Sir, yes, sir!

PRIVATE BROWN: The private has a father and stepfather that serve in the Air Force.

(*At 08:00 hours, we all marched to the parade deck. All stopped and stood at attention while the colors fly. On the main deck, over three thousand or more men and women fall in uniform formation. Generals, base commanders, coronels, majors, captains, gunnery sergeant, all the way down to privates. First Battalion, Platoon 1012, was one of many who knew how work together as a unit.*)

D & R Motorcycles

From a lad in England, I had always had a thing for motors on bikes. Sergeant Parker had got a 1.5 horsepower wheel which could be placed on any rear wheel of a bike and go from zero to thirty miles an hour very quickly. It was my first experience with a clutch with a lever to engage the device to three speeds. It was a blast. It ran on a one-fourth gallon of gas. Later in life, my life in mechanics would skyrocket with using my GI bill. I would enter national technical schools and get an associate degree—associate in science in automotive diagnostics and a certified lube technician from the Automotive Oil Change Association. After leaving the school and no longer staying with my cousin Katt, I lived and worked for a motorcycle shop called D & R—the names of two brothers, white guys who only worked on motorcycles. In fact, the star of the movie *Biker Boys* had upgrades done to his bike at D & R.

It was also the last time. I was able to see and visit Muhammad Ali's home by working on his motorcycle. In 1984, the Olympics were held in Los Angeles, and with all the extra-overcrowded freeways, motorcycles were the best way of transportation if you wanted to get somewhere in a hurry.

My job was fixing flats using an international tire-changing machine, oil changes, brakes, and engine breakdown. And when things got slow, I would work as a messenger for a service company, picking up and dropping off small items, like taking tickets to Michael Jackson's home and other stars who wanted small things in a hurry. The company was located in Century City. The great thing about bike shops was being able to drive all kinds of different bikes every day. I could drive bikes one hundred miles per hour down the freeway like I were Superman, and it never crossed my mind that I could hurt or kill myself with one wrong move against thousands of nutty drivers who don't give a damn about bikers. Hell, I drove a 350 cc Honda from Los Angeles to Sacramento one summer. The bike was so small, big trucks would shift me from land to another lane just by the force and speed of the wave of air passing by me. Yes! I had big balls and a small brain. Even some of the bigger bikes (CB650) had points that could get wet and not fire in the rain.

Definitely, Maybe

I was casted as a teacher in a TV pilot in which I was upgraded from a background actor to a day player. It was my first movie where I was given lines, and then I was a union must join because of the Taft-Hartley Act. The production company tried to screw me and didn't give me a contract even after I did the work. But I knew if I spoke words on film I was due one, but I played dumb and played their game. But after that show was wrapped, I went to the Screen Actors Guild and filled out a form. Once they (SAG) heard my voice in the dailies, they came with a contract and about $900 for the under-five bit. After that show, I got five union voters on the *Scorpion King 2*. There was a movie under the same name *Definitely, Maybe*, where the main actor was asked if she would go to the prom. While she enters the bus, she answers, "Definitely, maybe." I had worked for about twenty years as a background actor and met most of the major stars on set in those days. I never thought that I would ever join the union (SAG). But not only did I join SAG, I ran for president against the late Ken Howard two times.

Black or White

What is the color of love? I never thought I would ever have a white girlfriend until I went to England. Her name was Jane, and she had long brown hair. We didn't have sex, but I did get to second base with her. The girl I had in high school, Sue Smith, was a blonde bombshell. We were both virgins, and blood was left in the sleeping bag that hot summer night. I had a white girl at Evergreen State.

College in the black? Power days and the black sisters wouldn't give you no play, and they got upset when white women gave you some split tail. I ended up with a black girl, and I was okay with that because the white girls in college wanted to have sex so much until your penis became raw. They could never get enough. At first, it was exciting, but after a week of all night, you just want some rest. My brother and two of my sisters married white folks. My older sister married a teacher, and I respect and treat him like family because I know he loves my sister. My brother's wife is white, and he has been married for forty-two years. Her dad was black, and her mother was white. I had problems with Sue Smith's dad. He didn't like blacks, but her brother was cool with it!

Sister Souljah's Dream

I met the bright and talented sister late in my life. Once you read her books, you can't put them down. She is strong, smart, outspoken, yet kind and witty. At the book signing, she spoke of making a movie out of her book *The Coldest Winter Ever*, which was right up my alley as the Queen and I were both actors. Queen was a model and very attractive, short but like TNT-explosive. As a Muslim man, Sister Souljah appealed to the manhood of black men to love and protect women and kids. In my own life, there is a parallel of Midnight, the main character in her book, and me. We both are in love with two women at the same time. I am not married to them, but the deep love is still there all the same.

Koko dark-skinned, tall, with a strong body. She is business-minded. Her bloodline is from Haiti. Her body is shaped like an hour glass. She has large breasts and a smile that looks like stars. She is from Boston, educated, mild-manned, soft-spoken.

Jada is the second love. She is a light-skinned model from New York, street-wise, loud, smart, high fashion, emotional, smokes weed, high energy, sexy like a diamond.

Both women live for the LA dream, and both live in high-crime zones. All I can do is make sure they survive their environment and chase our dreams as actors in the Hollywood limelight.

Sister Souljah's story of the inner city and being a person of color with a different belief system is amazing.

Back To Basics: Killers in the Corps

PRIVATE SHERMAN: Where are you from, Brownie?

PRIVATE BROWN: Sacramento via Washington State. I was going to college up there!

PRIVATE SHERMAN: Wow, I tried to stay on your heels in that three-mile run.

PRIVATE BROWN: Stop smoking those Marlboros, fool! I'm the old man here at twenty-three! But I was a track man in high school. I'm not going to let that DI run my dick in the dirt.

PRIVATE SHERMAN: We run everywhere and then march the rest of the time!

PRIVATE BROWN: I hope I don't screw up the drills. Some of the assholes in here are into the blanket parties and hazing!

PRIVATE SHERMAN: What the fuck are hazing!

PRIVATE BROWN: Initiation rituals. I saw a private pushed in a locker for screwing up a drill. The buttheads closed the locker and set it on fire with lighter fluid while he was inside. I don't know why they did it, but I don't feel safe around some of these assholes!

PRIVATE SHERMAN: Copy that. Don't worry, Brownie. I got your six. Your mom made some good cookies. It reminded me of my home, and I am homesick right now.

PRIVATE BROWN: You are pretty cool for a white dude. I thought you would be fuck up coming from the south!

PRIVATE SHERMAN: I've seen that shit all my life. It ain't me. But what the fuck is a blanket party!

PRIVATE BROWN: You're like that dude Tom Hayden. He was an anti-war activist. He did a lot of good things for the people. He was down with good people like Doctor King! He is what my generation wanted for the world. Imagine that! Anyway, if you screw up on a drill, at night some dickheads throw a blanket over your head, and they pound on your head as payback.

PRIVATE SHERMAN: Damn, that fuck up! Does the DI know?

PRIVATE BROWN: I don't give a shit if they do. Cover my six, and I got your back.

Private Sherman: Cool, brother, you got my word!

PRIVATE BROWN: Great! If we help each other, we can get past all this bullshit.

PRIVATE SHERMAN: I needed a job, and I had a run-in with the law. That's why I am here!

PRIVATE BROWN: Well, I bet you didn't know that some of these guys are killers who will see the frontlines, and they don't give a damn about you or me, so stay alert and sleep with one eye open!

PRIVATE SHERMAN: Okay! Why killers?

PRIVATE BROWN: Because if they come back for Nam, they will get a pardon!

Hollywood (Where Dreams Are Made)

People come from all over the world to see the magic of Hollywood, the Walk of Fame, like my acting teacher Lawrence Merrick used to say, "Hollywood controls the minds of the world. And you as actors can be a big part of it!" He was a genius! A very bright man. "O slave of desire, Float upon the stream. Little spider, stick to your web. Or else abandon your sorrows for the way" ("Desire" from the Dhammapada).

"Acting is a complex and elusive art to define. Yet almost everyone can tell good acting from bad acting- or good acting from brilliant acting. Why can one actor be riveting in a play and another actor be dull and boring in the very same play, doing the same character, the same lines? If it were just the script, the beauty of its language, the artful turn of a phrase, we would only need reading. But the words are not just read with sterility from the page. They are performed and brought to life by actors" (*The Power of the Actor*, Ivana Chubbuck).

The American Public

Those who have never been to Europe don't understand how the folks in the United Kingdom roll and the rest of Europe and parts of Africa. They drive on the opposite side of the road. And the same is true of the driver's wheel, which is placed on the other side of the car, where the passenger sits. And most cars still use a clutch because it saves on gas, and because the transmission is in line with the road traction. There is more control when going uphill or downhill for the experienced driver. On a motorcycle, popping the clutch can lift the front very quickly. With balance you can perform a wheelie.

With a heavy-duty clutch, you can burn rubber in all gears in a high-performance car. My first real car was a 1957 Chevrolet Bel Air, black and white. And then there was a 1969 Fleetwood Cadillac, 500 cu in displacement. The Chevrolet had a 409 cu in displacement. Both cars were fast. They would pass everything on the road except a gas station. I had more sex in the Cadillac than I did in a motel. The 1957 was so fast with a stick I did burn rubber in all four gears. Real carburetors, steel heads and body. Those were the good old days. We didn't have seat belts, balls to the wall!

Jimi Marshall "Jimi" Hendrix

November 27 is a day when Bruce Lee and Jimi Hendrix share, and they both are laid to rest in the same city—Seattle, Washington. I was living in England at the time when I first saw Jimi on a British TV program called the *Top of the Pops* and on a show called *Ready, Steady, Go!* He was on fire. The energy was above the charts. I followed him back to the United States when most of my generation was still into soul music, and Motown, and even surf music. I had seen and loved all the leaders of rock, the Who, the Animals, Kinks Yardbirds, Dave Clark Five, the Beatles, Rolling Stones, Herman Hermits, Cream, and of course Jimi Hendrix.

There was only one African-American in my high school who loved rock music the way I loved rock. His name was Allen Lewis. Everyone else had no idea who Jimi was, or he didn't really interest them. But my white girlfriend, Sue Smith, got me a record for my birthday. It was Janis Joplin and Big Brother Holding Company. That was so sweet, so I got her tickets to see Jimi at the California State Fair. We smoked weed and freaked out on the sounds. The first time I saw Jimi live was at the Sacramento Memorial Auditorium, where I worked as an usher. I loved that job because I saw many great artists of that era.

James Brown, Three Dog Night, Bill Hailey and the Comets, the Platters, Peter, Paul and Mary, Bo Diddley, Arthur Brown, Steppenwolf, Chuck Berry, and others. To watch Jimi play was surreal even without taking drugs; you were high as a kite.

Many people come to Hollywood with big dreams but no plan to combat this network of trial and error to have the spotlight shine bright on their acting skills and hard work as day players. Luck and knowing the right people can help, but you must still be prepared. Koko is a very sexy, hard-working, black, and attractive female who has a "work hard," "nose to the grindstone," "leave no rock unturned" approach to working in the industry and becoming an actor who has paid dues to make things happen. Her easygoing personality can be a problem at times in this "dog eat dog" world of casting call and call backs. You have to push her at times to make her fight. She has to learn how not to be too nice. And she has to learn to take risks at times because she is super careful about all affairs. I love her because she is so kind. She is a smart lady who demands respect and honor. I don't want to change her but help her whenever I can, actor to actor, woman to man.

The 50th Law

"The greatest fear people have is that of being themselves. They want to be 50 Cent or someone else. They do what everyone else does even if it doesn't fit where and who they are. But you get nowhere that way; your energy is weak and no one pays attention to you. You are running away from the one thing that you own what makes you different. I lost that fear. And once I felt the power that I had by showing the world I didn't care about being like other people, I could never go back" (50 Cent).

Hollywood Magic versus Malcolm X

Al Hajj Malik Shabazz (1925–1965), RIP. A few days ago, my relative asked me for advice about his personal problems. Like most black men in our community, he has been led to the incorrect ways of living and not following the wisdom of God (Allah), and as a result, it increases their problems—drinking, not drinking clean water, not reading books, not working out at the gym, drugs, not getting eight hours of rest, not eating the proper foods. Malcolm X had the same life habits when he was a young man. But he overcame his personal problems, lack of education, knowledge of self and kind and became a leader, helping black men to not be the evil spells of Hollywood. This is your role model to correct your problems of life. None of the TV or movies people today in popular culture are following God's calling; they are following Satan.

Back to Basics (Part 2)

All the men marched to the training course, which has large dummies hanging for different drills. A drill instructor dressed in all green began to give us lessons in martial arts and hand-to-hand combat. I had training from a master from Korea who trained student at Evergreen State. The hammer fist, front snap kick, different blocks, tiger stance, etc. were already a part of my training.

The Korean tae kwon do has rules of etiquette that the Marine Corps had no regard for, no real discipline rules or courtesy.

STAFF SERGEANT CLAY: Each of you will be given a slice of this rubber hose!

PRIVATE SHERMAN: Sir, what does the private do with this?

STAFF SERGEANT CLAY: Private Brown, about-face!

(*I followed orders and turned around.*)

STAFF SERGEANT CLAY: Private Sherman, place that hose above Brownie's Adam's apple and choke him out. Now, Private, pressure!

Private Sherman used the hose around my neck with force and pressure until I was unconscious. I was unconscious for a least three minutes. I lay down in the hot dirt, air returning to my lungs. I was surprised that this was part of my training. When I was in high school playing baseball, a student hit me in the head with a baseball bat. That was the first time I was totally unconscious; this was the second time!

Lucy, the Daughter of the Devil: Human Sacrifice

Was a play at the Bohemian Grove! Orion was my deepest relative besides my uncle Richard who didn't believe in God. Orion is a prominent constellation located celestial equator and visible throughout the world.

Orion in my life was a proud African Jew. He became very aware of insight in the world. Orion had explained the secret players behind that world stage. Orion has twenty-five years of research on UFOs, and he would tape ships in the air. He thought one day a mother ship would come to earth, pick up 144,000, and destroy the white man's earth. Orion was one in a million. He wasn't afraid to tell it like it is. Orion speaks with confidence about bizarre subjects, and if you didn't agree or know the subject, he would just move on. He didn't like white Jesus, and he would say that whenever the word Jesus is mentioned in a movie, somebody always dies. He gave me all kinds of books on Masonic and the occult, which explained the real rules of this world and their evil plans.

He explained the illuminati to me! The real jet-black ones to the grafted current ones. Orion was the one who told me about a UFO in the sixties. He said the government shot rounds of ammunition at the object before it took off. The weapons killed some folks on the ground. Orion knew the truth of the 9/11 questions, because he always questions.

A Kid in an English Candy Store

Rowntrees Jelly Tots, Fruit Pastilles, Fruit Gums, Maltesers, After Eight Mints, Coffee Crisp, Wispa Milk Coffee Crisp, Wispa Milk Chocolate Bars, cream fudge, fudge, caramel wafer biscuits, Milky Bar, Blue Riband, Dairy Milk barfi, fruit-and-nut bars, Penguin, Topic, Fry's Chocolate Cream, Lion Mars, York Sherbet, Trebor, Polo, Murray Mints, Refreshers, Double Lollies, Galaxy, Bounty, etc., etc.

And of course, we blokes must have our bloody tea. Typhoo, Typhoo Decaf, white tea, Tetley Decaf, PG decaf for starts. Then HP Sauce, HP Fruity, Heinz Salad Cream for meats, and Heinz Beans to make you fart.

When I lived in our small cottage with the shelter in the front yard about a mile away, we walked by the cow pastures past the footpaths. They used to have houses with store fronts. This was an excellent chance for me to use British currency. The pound was five American dollars at that time. A shilling was a coin worth one-twentieth of a pound. The British slang for a pound is called quid. You cellars were useless in England unless you have an exchange as a young lad. And there were no large supermarkets at that time in England. You could go to a farmers market and see rabbits hanging and fresh fish on ice.

Quail is a bird that tastes wonderful with their breasts cooked in butter in the small pan. It was wonderful as a kid to see different peoples, places, and things. The candy shop was my sweetest weakness. I lost my teeth later due to all the spoils of candy. And I loved every minute of it. My mouth would water over the different kinds of candies, teas, dressing for meats. Eating a three-minute egg with tea and toast started our day of proper, a super day!

Worcestershire was on most English tables and maybe HP. Most English folk are very friendly to travelers. Think about it the next time you see people from a place far away. Your communication is highlighted to be understood loud and clear. I had good teachers in England, and I was the best of students. *Not!* I can never repay the woman who lived next door for helping me understand the basics of English grammar and history (England and American) and some math and science. And my teacher for math.

You always got better service in a store from home. You face has more value, not like when you in a supermarket and you're just a number. Every person adds value. I loved the wine gums; they were special! And let's not forget the fruit-and-nut bar; it holds a place in my heart. Bloody right, mate.

The mornings in England were fresh. The air is always moist. The milk man would leave six bottles of real milk with the cream being at the very top, just right for tea or coffee.

Screen Actors Strike

I never imagined after almost twenty years of doing background work as a Hollywood extra that I would ever be a member of the union. Not only did I become a member of the Screen Actors Guild. I ran for office of president against the late Ken Howard, who was a Jew, with charm and wit. He was the force for the merger with AFTRA. I was against the merger because AFTRA was in deep debt. Alan Rosenberg was also against it. He was the former president, and he had no problems with a strike who was anti-union. Ken was giving away to AFTRA, and his Republican running mate from Orange County really pissed me off! I had to ask the membership for their signatures to run for office. Ken had other members do it for him. Ken had it like that. Alan had lead a strike that lasted more than fifty days and hurt a lot of folks, but he was determined not to give in. Good for him! A rebel and a fighter. Ken was a pawn for the status quo and pushed the merger. After my three defeats to the known likeable actor, I knew he was sick, but when he died, it took me by surprise!

So the new president called a strike for a new contract in 2016. I was saying this might not have happened if Ken was living. At this time, I wanted to join the rank-and-file members with Dave White and the elite, but my foot had a cast, and I couldn't get it wet because of the rain. But the second strike day, my cast was gone, and I went even if I couldn't walk. I gave moral support to the membership as they marched around me on the ground. They organized from a marine point of view, but they did speak and act like one unit. After all my days as a member of SAG-AFTRA, this was a good day. Not since the sixties had I felt so much a part of a group that worked together for our same goals and dreams for our future.

Splash

A black face goes down deep inside a four-foot-deep pool, along with the rest of the company. DI was screaming, "Swim to the other side and back, private." I was again lucky I had taken swimming since I was a kid and took some more classes in college. Even with all that training, I drank a lot of the pool, more than I wanted to. When you are swimming in a wet uniform, you must use a lot of force and energy to propel your face and body in the water. Catching your air between strokes and kicking forward. The DI screamed, "Keep the fuck moving! Move! Move!"

Finally, I hit the other wall, returning for the home stretch, the last full length of the pool, stroking . . . like a machine. Drinking less water, arms can lift slowly, stroke hit the wall and out marine exploration. There are three things that go a long way in the corps: (1) you are good firing weapons, (2) you are a good swimming in water, (3) you can run quickly and for a long distance if need be!

"They are afraid of lovebecause love is something they can't control."

Many of you don't recall or remember a movie about Big Brother. The movie was called *Big Brother's Hallmark Show*, 1984. And just like in the movie, Big Brother is watching you even in your sleep. There is no danger of the ruling class being deposed. "Nothing is ever hidden from the thought police." The 1984 movie told of a police state, minded control total, where love between a man and woman is not allowed. Hate is the motivation behind their actions! "Freedom is slavery," the signs say. War is peace. The more things change, the more they stay the same. You love your country, you send the kids off to war, for a demonic system, for the evildoers on this planet. The power of love was the message in the music of Jimi. The power of love is stronger than hate. You can take to the bank. The matrix can't exist in love. Healing takes place when souls connect to other souls, peaceful and soft undertones of emotions. Quiet and peaceful. Smoking herbal can bend the mind toward peace. Drive your mind to a different awareness. You begin to understand the fundamentals of being human.

What a wonderful world was a song Louis Armstrong's hit song telling of a different wonderful people loving people. This kind of world is not the red pill or the matrix. That is the world the evildoers want. We want peace and love; the rulers could care less. They don't care about money. They have more money than God. They want complete power and control of the whole world and to make slaves out the whole human race. "They are afraid of love because love is something they can't control." They don't want you to connect to the cosmos, to find out that you are a part of everything. They teach you how to think, not to think! You are a genius, and you forgot that you are. They want to keep your mind in an eggshell, never realizing the real power you have over your life. Look at the facts. The facts are reality, questions. There is no such thing as a dumb question.

Most of the things they tell you are mixed with lies, and they have no proof to back the stories told. Orion told me to question everything, look at the hidden meaning in symbols they put it in books, movies, sellevision, billboards, etc.

They put it right in your face, but you are too dumb to see the message. They have taken away your identity. You don't think for yourself. You are programed how to think and what to buy, feel, and act. Feel free to free yourself. You are you own master!

Innocence of Childhood

A picture of snowcapped mountains. Thousands of clouds high kissing mountaintops. Snow drifts, and clouds blend in a sea of tranquility. A valley of high clouds for as far as the eyes could see. On top of the mountains, snow banks hundreds of feet high. In 1951, *Red Skelton*, *Kukla, Fran and Ollie*, and *Captain Video* were shows that stand out for a kid. *Amos 'n' Andy* on CBS was high-rated. *The Lone Ranger* was on kids' top seed. But I did watch *Hopalong Cassidy*, the number one on the rated show, and *I Love Lucy*, with her son having the same as mine, family time. Everyone called me Ricky in those days. And Ricky loved Jackie Gleason. He was CBS big star and that leaves me with the *$64,000 Question*, which *Dragnet* could never solve.

The world wasn't in peace then, and "Will we ever see world peace?" is the question that must be asked for our children's sake. The scientist said we only have a thousand years before the world falls apart. By that time, we humans have a chance to survive, which is about six light years away on a world ten times bigger than ours—at least that is what the super brains say!

No Show for Grandbaby

So today, I will meet my grandson, a new part of the story of my life. It's exciting to imagine that a part of me will continue in the river of life. I must try to master myself and keep an open mind. Time has shown me many faces. The passage of change from boyhood to man, to father, to grandfather. And it all comes with a price. So will I be a wise man or a fool in relationship of this human experience? No female committed, like in the traditional role of man and woman. I musty refine and maintain control of emotion, try to break new grounds. Attack and counterattack must be checked.

I warn folks of painful remarks and don't reveal my real feeling. It's pouring rain now, and my grandson never showed up! Wow! I took my first step without crutches today. My first since the operation. I'm happy about that. Not being able to use my foot has been a learning experience. You find out who your real friends are, and that's a good thing. Surgery was very painful, and now my life is heading in a positive direction. I'm glad it's starting to heal.

Marine Corps Flag versus Confederate Flag

The military's colors are red, white, and blue. But some white Marines cross the line with the confederate flag hanging out their back pockets. They don't care if blacks are offended as they came down the line in the chow hall. I won't serve them, and I was never punished for not serving them. I was just an enlisted man, but I'm sure that officers above me saw the flags and their non-actions could only mean that they were with the rebels. But I had to face the reality of their actions. Did it hurt my feeling? Yes! But I got over it and just did my job. I had the same uneasy feeling when I was overseas in Japan. Two white Marines, every word out of their mouth was "Gook this" or "Gook that." Their racism was on point-blank blast. So I knew how they felt about blacks. So I won't talk much and remain silent. It reminded me of a time in Seattle when the man who lived next door nabbed a man burning a cross in our lawn. He was arrested, but the impact was still there. See evil for evil and good for good.

All the small-mind thinking, I didn't really care about; I had already represented my country overseas before in the United Kingdom, and I would not disrespect a host nation or its people. A visitor should understand and be friendly to people of other nations. White racism is a mental issue. You hate someone by their skin color. That same person may save your life, dumbass. Fools are running the world. The world is so advanced, yet there is so much darkness.

Holidays

PRIVATE BROWN: The USO is giving letters to the troops. I think everyone knows it's tough to be far away from home for the holidays!

PRIVATE HOLIDAY: Yo, Brother Brown, it's like I told you, every day is a holiday and every meal is a feast if you wake up and you're six feet above ground.

PRIVATE BROWN: Thanks, I don't think I will ever forget your words (*I thought to myself.*)

PRIVATE SHERMAN: I'm going to buy a set of dress blues.

PRIVATE BROWN: I'm jealous! I sure can't afford them. I have to send money home.

PRIVATE SHERMAN: Yeah, bro, they cost like three hundred bucks at the PX. Some people got it like that!

PRIVATE HOLIDAY: No funds can hold a brother back, but holiday really means freedom from work.

PRIVATE BROWN: Vacation.

PRIVATE HOLIDAY: Exactly.

PRIVATE BROWN: I never thought I would be like a soldier like in a Disney movie or like the Marines are part of the Hollywood Christmas Parade, like forever!

PRIVATE SHERMAN: They give away toys to kids every year, and that's a good thing.

PRIVATE BROWN: The evolution from boyhood to manhood is exciting.

PRIVATE HOLIDAY: Brother Brown, I know you feel bad that you'll never own a pair of dress blues.

PRIVATE BROWN: You asshole.

PRIVATE HOLIDAY: You have been a prick since the Marine Corps birthday, Veteran's Day, and now here we go again.

PRIVATE BROWN: Sorry, guys, I get this fucked-up feeling every blue moon. I really feel bad about my girl back home. She is a thing I can't get out of my head. And now with a baby here, it's hard to think straight without all the emotions to deal with.

For Your Eyes Only (Part 2)

Ron Glass and Jim Kelly were black actors who were prime from my generation. Both are cool brothers, if you were lucky enough to meet them. But like I said, Muhammad Ali was the greatest star in my lifetime, and he can't be replaced ever. Every place in the world knew him. I can't believe it was eight years ago since I worked with Ron Glass. We ate dinner with Kerry Washington on set. I had met Kerry a few days before at an award show in Santa Monica. Ron was cast as her father, while Samuel L. Jackson played the crazy black cop who lived next door. I was thinking about Ron and got side-tracked by Kerry. One of the best views of her body is her legs and of course her face.

Jim Kelly was the first black movie star I met in Hollywood. I would run into him at the health food store. He was the grand master par excellence. They both were true professional about their craft. I learned a lot from these brothers. I am glad we crossed paths. Him and others like Robin Harris.

Robin and I used to play ball for hours at Hollywood Recreation Center back in the day. Robin had worked with Spike Lee movie *Do the Right Thing*. Robin was known for Baby Baby Kids. Speaking of back in the day, I used to go to the same acting school with Tony Cox.

Tony Cox, who is a Hollywood star and has been for a number of years now. It is good to see actors you know skyrocket from Merrick Studios. The smallest actor is now the tallest actor. And the giant beside him is about to fall. Stand, stand, stand!

It seemed as if I had a block toward writing, and with the TV programs and the news and other things, one cannot master your own thoughts. So the master must become silent and see the mind pure. It's great to be fluid. I'm turning sixty-five soon, and I'm still fighting. Being disabled for a while was a mind-altering experience.

You really can't take anything for granted. Writing this book has been a dream come true. I'm not trying to be Sister Souljah; I knew in a New York second that she is a lot smarter than your kid, so I still can learn a lot from her. She gave her speech standing room only. She signed my book *A Moment of Silence*. It was in December, the same week as my birthday. She is a very witty, aware, and hip black woman.

Who can control his or her thoughts and slow down? The body used to move fast. Not so fast now. You don't go anywhere without restrictions. The mind is willing, but the flesh is weak. Stream of thoughts and ideal questions. Can I reach higher planes? Can I control my mind in words, thoughts, and deeds? This is the inner part of the book that expands your mind, you the reader. Slow down, relax, be at peace with yourself. How can you learn if you don't quiet your mind? Be still. Be quick to do good. Be slow to act a damn fool. Yeah! I can't fuck around now in life. I got kids, grandkids, and great-grandkids. So you better make wise decisions, old man.

The Best Christmas Ever

It only happens every year, SAG-AFTRA Christmas party and the birthday boy, *moi*. In an actor's life, it's rare when things in life align up and the cosmos works in your favor. Last year was dull. I took another female actor. The results were much different, and that's the past.

So this year was special because of the footwork done and the lack of being mobile. Nevertheless, the paying my dues as a member, working with other actors going on strike supporting our common goals in one voice. And the sweet part was at the end of the year, Koko was there. She did a lot of good acting work and was offered an acting job in the lobby, waiting to enter. She came from Boston, and within a few years, she has reached the core of actors in Hollywood perfect! A wonderful party, and Koko and I enjoyed the food, and the actors are superb. I am happy!

I turned sixty-five in a few days, and I am thankful to be alive, not taking anything for granted. She was a major part of me, getting back on my feet, and I have to give credit to the other female actor last year; she helped too. She is a good look and can cook. I think that this year was better for me.

Gang Starr

My son and I worked with Gang Starr back in 1998. Ricky is the boy who is enclosed by a futuristic cops. You know my Steez video "Much Love." You can see it on YouTube. I was not interested that much by rap music at that time. Mad skills with the mike, positive messages. This group had a lot of different ideas and expressed them loud and clear.

Sixty-Five and Alive

Wow! I'm at an age of human life span, having a full life. Ups and downs, breakthroughs, and setbacks, all in a mad, mad, mad, mad, mad world. Now I am a senior in very sense of the word. And we all know the seniors rule the school. It's the last of school that we all must face. The wonderful life has shown many faces and many of my kin and friends have seen death's face and have expired. I used to be quick, speedy fast, running, riding motorcycles and cars, and racing at high speeds, but now I know I got a lot of miles, running in life. It's all gone now!

I am thankful to have seen all those days. Many moons have passed, and the mind did grow and the body too. I just wish sometimes I had this worldly knowledge when I was younger. I could have saved myself a lot of heartfelt problems with the skills of learning and communication as a student and sometimes a teacher of life. Being in the human family can be wonderful at times. I can still try to be my own master, which is something I've learned over time. It's great to go back to silence and try to control my mind. If my body is slow, I must slow down my mind also until they are one.

Today Freddy troubleshot a car using his circuit testing probe. We tested the electrical system until we found out it was a blower relay in the heating and the AC unit was defective. The heater blower is working, just the relay was bad. I still need more tools at sixty-five!

It's been many years since I was wearing the uniform. But all Marines know the rules don't change. America is our home. Freedom is not always given to all people. And that's not justice.

Our awareness is coming to light, the young people get uprooted by the same old tricks. Being in the Marines is not like a John Wayne movie. War is real, and you can't be replaced. War is hell; that can never be repeated enough, but someone will always play the warrior. The brotherhood is hard core.

2016

After the death of Muhammad Ali and Ken Howard and many other stars pass in the bye and bye, Ken was talked about at the SAG-ATRA Christmas party. Carrie Fisher, her mother, and many other would soon follow. Without a doubt, this year will stand out. Time is flying like Superman, faster than a speeding bullet. Hollywood and the world are in deep sorrow and sadness. They have entered the black hole of the universe. Never to return. Nothing will last forever. Not even the sun. We are all over time in a mad, mad, mad, mad, mad world. Year 2016 was a test-full year. Even in my own life, my works were varied and interesting. As an actor, being in at least one film that should be released soon, my ego has a little lift. It is what it is; one thousand years from now, it will be meaningless as money given to a pig.

Veteran Homeless

LA was bragging about how they were having less homeless veterans. But then a vet ran up to the mike and said there was a homeless camp under the under pass near the freeway. You can go anywhere downtown and see vets sleeping under a cardboard box or a tent.

The public doesn't understand what it is like to be a veteran. Then they say hire the vet, but it doesn't help them with jobs, housing, food, or emotional support. All those words like "Thank you for your service" are heard few and far between if at all. Staying in a shelter is a bad joke. The smell of piss and standing with people who don't understand how to be clean, I would rather sleep in my truck or van than to sleep uneasy with gunshots fired in the downtown area loaded with gangs and a skid row killer who was around at that time. Thanks but no thanks. We vets were told we were on a list for housing for vets. Right! The list had folks (us) for five years.

In the news, a veteran killed innocent folks at the airport.

Wow! Hell, what was his state of mind? How is he compared to the other veteran killers? How is he the same? What makes a man kill harmless people? And it always gets back to peace, with the words of the master saying that it is the foolish one who follows impure thoughts. At first the fruit of his deeds don't bear fruit, but then the foolish disappears, and karma takes effect. Boom! "Reality has a way with catching up with you." This is a quote from President Obama in his farewell speech in 2017.

Now I have seen the change of an era. As a young black man, it was impossible to see black heroes, and many so-called Negros didn't want to be black. But since I was a kid, we had stand-up black heroes, King and Ali. Later there were many others to look up to. A black president has a great impact, and with family. A real role model. This alone is progress. So in a real way, times have changed. To have a black president is a game changer. Too bad the first family didn't have a male child. But it is what it is!

Dream Girl

So the idea of desire and attachment and dealing with time and life and women. We as men must deal with the acts and the facts that even if we had our dream girl, there will be attraction problems and/or disinterest. My relationships with women have changed so much over the years. I've come into the world and had sex with women, had children by women, and now having grandkids. I spend a lot of time thinking about women and how I can improve myself when dealing with them.

I heard news that my real father was about to lose his leg. I wish my father was close, but that's not the case, even if he is the only earthy father who got me into this wonderful world. I have learned to be my own man now at this point in life. I have learned to live without his love, so now is my idea to return that love or not to do anything at all. It's kind of like getting dumped by an old girlfriend. The more you try to chase the woman for attraction, the more she does not have shit to do with you and you have no idea why. I guess I should be happy as most black kids don't know their fathers. And he did teach me how to fish. Which was important as a kid. My dad most likely greet you with "Hey, fella, how have you been?"

My sister called and told me about the operation to remove his leg. "Papa, don't take no mess" had to do it on the good foot. It seems like women have my mind bonded in soft chains, but they are chains just the same.

Well, the actor Betty White turned ninety-five today. And she is still working. That's good news for all old actors. I worked with her on some show back in the day. And my mother just told me that my grandmother was born on the 26th of January and my brother has gone back to Sacramento to see about our father.

If I were to go to Sacramento, I would have to drive in the rain as storms much needed came through California. And people in LA can barely drive when it is dry, and every time it rains, at least eight hundred auto crashes happen. People speed faster on oil and water, and some cars have bald tires and bad breaks pads. I want to be able to control my emotions and try to master myself! But it's so hard when you are dealing with a live person. So it must be game on from now on! I went to be more mindful of how I act around others (i.e., women). I forget a lot of times that I even have a female side of myself. The male in me is always the side of me that is grounded.

The female side is full of power with creative energy. I'm still trying to figure out what life is all about at sixty-five. I'm moving fast in my mind, but the body is wearing out, and what can one do with that reality? I went back to the gym the other day, and now my muscles hurt so I will go back tomorrow. I've stopped working at the auto auction. Now we have a new president. All these years, we talked about the new world order to all my friends and family after Barry, my cousin, left the world a few years ago. We warned everyone to hear only quiet conservative views and ask God to help you get by.

David Icke told the public that America's congress has the symbols for fascism in the congress offices, and like Maxwell Jordon said, most of the public see these of power but don't know what they represent. Perception deception. *Precept* is "a rule or principle imposing a particular standard or conduct." *Deception* is "the fact or state of being deceived." David says that people are opening up their minds. They are going beyond Jew, Muslim, black, white, etc. and opening up their minds.

Control people's perception, and you control their information. Fake news comes out of nowhere. It is all a game of the mind. Don't question the information because it not dealing with the truth. Suppress information because it not dealing with truth. Suppress information because you are scared of it. Reality is an illusion, but it is a persistent one. Jordon Maxwell says the Award show run by the National Academy of Television Arts and Sciences spells Satan backward. The magic wand that was Disney is the wand made by the Hollywood tree, and in their race is the bloodline of animals. "If you don't stand for something, you will fall for anything."

Pawns in the Game

Alex Jones went deep inside the Bohemian Grove they stayed one hundred years ago. Presidents, bankers, the Hollywood elite. One-world government, deep occultist, and they do ritual with a human sacrifice with homosexual porn stars with high-powered people (322) of the church of Satan, blue lodge, thirty-three degrees, and Albert Pike, the head of the Klan, the knight of the Secret Circle. Secret Society was formed to kill, steal, and destroy.

Watch Trump get party up is not happening, yet I'm curious just to see. "I came, I saw, I conquered." Trumps works and words. Unspoken words. It seems to me that all the stories in these years and movies are basically the same. Some writers write volumes in a short time. I am not one of them.

So watching the Marines guard all the president's men doing their jobs regardless of political views. The protest have never happened for this event or this scale. Like I said before the election, I told my cousin Cathy, who supported Hilary, that I saw Trump signs everywhere, the farmers on the Golden State to Sacramento and Vallejo. My other cousin Janice, who is a lawyer, didn't give a damn. What do you have when you have ten thousand lawyers in the bottom of the sea? I don't know, but it a good start!

Sunday 22, 2017. Well, it's early Sunday morning. I call my mother every Sunday for at least twenty years now, and she likes it. We keep up with the family through her. That's how important she is to the family! It's raining again in Los Angeles. Last week, it was the King Parade, which was positive and peaceful this year compared to last few years. And this week, we have a new president and a huge protest against it. We, Mom and I, like to talk about basketball. Her team is the Warriors, and I like Oklahoma. And since her team are the ex-champions, we have things to talk about. I remember now all my years of homelessness and how it doesn't make me feel human to have people look down on you, and you push back as much as you can. Sleeping in your car was a blessing. At least I had a car to sleep in. Living outdoors doesn't work at all. I'm glad the past has changed. Now I wonder about the future. My acting value has decreased with age. And with an X factor in the white house, one only wonders what the future holds for a brother. I'm still in love with Koko, but I know she has another man. It was raining too much for her not to have one over the past two years. I've gotten close, but I want more, yet I'm afraid to commit to action. But this year maybe is my last chance to have a mate. I must make up my mind to set up a deadline for her, because I know of all the women out there, she rates number 1. Wow! Maybe my female sidekicks in me start writing more and can detail exposition. White power written on his face scared Mom at the Denny's Cafe. That was the first time she had seen a person with a gang identification. I told her that in LA I've seen a person I know who had fucked the police on the top of his forehead. *Now* the whole world sees the writing on the wall.

My mother also said she went to see her brother Joe, who is in my family. He has had mental problems for years since my grandmother's death. My brother said my dad's operation was good. If there is any good about losing your leg. But the bottom line is that he is still alive, and that is still something to be thankful for living! So I am assuming that Koko and Danielle were both at the march for women. And many hate men for standing up for their rights.

But the black women are not as educated about their history like sisters in the past were. I'm really enjoying writing this information down; it has to hold some positive effects. So my nature is to try to take advantage of whatever I can do at this point in my life. I'm glad I wanted to be an actor. It is the best job I have ever had. And the mechanical background is still the best way for gaining income to live. Winter wonderland in the mountains this year, we need it. Women love men they respect. Women love strong men, with confidence, boldness, emotional stability, purpose in life, strong drive, positive mind-set, healthy. This is a note to yourself. Women, thousands of them, last night were fighting for their rights. Cool! Time on the clock, in football and other games, is quoted. Women have made the higher ups to see their views. And I am the man with the golden typewriter. I recall that it rained today!

Women's Jail

I remember all the times I would go to the jail to visit her. To get her weight back to normal and get that ass fat again, instead of looking like a little boy with tits. She had a pretty face when we met at twenty-two, and she was killed by a hit-and-run driver. So sad. That was 2014. She was acting very strange a week before her death.

The Man with the Golden Typewriter (Part 2)

"I always knew I had it in me, and I forgive you all for all my pain." It is from the song about Muhammad Ali from the movie *The Greatest*. In the start of the movie, you see Ali in church with family with the white Christ in the background and racism gone wild everywhere. In the film, he throws his gold medal he won in Rome into the river. When asked why he threw it in the river, he said "It's phony, it ain't worth a damn."

He ran six miles each day. He didn't follow a blond-hair, blue-eyed Jesus. When asked why he didn't want to go to war for America, he says, "The Viet Cong is not my enemy they never called me a nigger!" All souls are near and dear to the creator. There ain't no red-neck cracker gonna run us out of here. Belinda, his wife, had a panic attack as Ali is beaten by Ken Norton.

Rain

I do recall on my tour in England in which you needed boots, hats, gloves, etc. In Seattle, it was about the same amount of rainfall. In college at Evergreen State, it rained so much we saved a smoke house on an Indian reservation from falling into the river. I welcome the rain now, but I do feel bad for the homeless and the poor. The rain cleans the air, which is important. It reminds of me of the time when baby was in my life. I miss her so much. I knew that our time together was special. I love her regardless of life doing whatever she wanted, regardless of what happens.

Marcus Aurelius, one of the great thinkers of antiquity, said, "A man's life is what his thoughts make of it." Ralph Waldo Emerson said, "A man is what he thinks about all day long." Every achievement in this world was projected as a creative idea. A famous psychologist says, "There is a deep tendency in human nature to be precisely like that which you habitually imagine yourself to be."

Straight Out of Central Casting

As a non-union background actor in the late seventies, work was everywhere. You could work sixty-plus hours a week, no problem. Central has been around for at least ninety years, and is the main supply of background actors for film and TV. Learning how to cross in front of a camera is one of the first joys of the industry. When you come to Hollywood and you are a new face, they want to put you on as many shows as possible.

When you master the experience of being on set and working with high-powered stars, doing their thing, you are there watching and learning and wondering, "Is this really real?"

If the casting director learns your face, and that is their job, you can work a ton of movies and sellevision shows.

I worked stand-in for Joe Morgan and Ron Glass. Working stand-in is always a higher-base pay. While on set, I even ran lines while they relaxed. Back in the day, if you had a Thomas map, a pager, a car that wasn't red, white, or black, the work was on and popping. I have met and worked with a lot of stars, and most of them are really nice people. Some are kind of strange, but most of them are good human being. They have problems, too, like everyone else. It's just on a larger scale. Thank you, Central Casting, for sending me on all these shows listed and some that are not.

The Tao of Central Casting
Strong Medicine
The West Wing
Definitely Maybe—pilot (day player)
Las Vegas—Sugar Shane Mosley's cut man
Judging Amy
Providence
Sweet Justice

Courthouse—Robert Givins
The Visitor
The Praa Practice
Space Jam
J.A.G.
NIKE
Three Sisters
Lady Killers
Skin
Yes, Dear
Nick of Time
Strange Days
Citizen Raines
Batman Returns
Bodyguard
Play Nice Intruders
FBI: The Untold Stories (stand-in)
Doogie Howser
Parker Lewis can't lose
Beverly Hills 90210
Love and War
Unlawful Entry
Mr. Baseball
Drexell's Class
Panther
Tour of Duty
Reasonable Doubts
Sister
Lethal Weapon 3
Murder She Wrote
Night Court
Mr. Jones
NYPD Blue
Babylon
Knots Landing
Final Shot

Seven Heaven
Thieves
Hard Times on Planet Earth
ER
Malcolm in the Middle
The Fighting Fit
Scorpion King
Life
The Division
Crazy as Hell
Family Law
Frank Mcklusky
CSI
K-PAX
A Few Good Hearts
Pay or Play
Chicago Hope
Iron Man 2
Star Trek: Into the Darkness
Oz the Great and Powerful

They are many shows to follow that are not listed.

Thanks to all the shows that gave me work and a chance to work with the biggest stars in the industry. And thanks goes out to Central Casting, Sande Allessi, Jeff Orlan, Rich King, and many others for their hard work over the years.

Be Quiet, Loving, and Fearless

Trevon Martin's death was five years old today. The parents are writing a book called *Rest in Power*. The mother tells how he was really a momma's boy, she used to call him cupcake. She misses so many things about him. He wanted to be an aviation mechanic, but he died at seventeen! Black Lives Matter formed after his death.

Being a person who was raised as a Catholic who also knew the whole mass in Latin. Long ago later changing to Islam and later in life, and now I feel bad for the people that have been killed in the mosque or church. How can you say you love God and do such a thing? Silence cannot make a master out of a fool!

I really don't understand how a man can kill innocent . . . and still expect to live to tell about it! If he were black, they would not take them alive. Why the double standard? If you are white, you have the law behind you. But I don't trust them hoes.

As the Super Bowl comes up, I remember having two females at the same time back in 2014. It seems like all females have a slut inside them, deep, deep inside. I'm seeking the truth behind the male-and-female game. But the truth is, a lot of females are sluts and love sex just as much as men do! They are looking for the right man to bring it out. A bad dream comes to the single man who finds out that he is just a friend. It's happen to me many times. I've been a wuss and have been tricked when I was young, but no more! I don't chase them hoes no more. It don't get you anywhere. I should have learned from my old slut. I miss her, but she was still a hoe. Anyway, the more you do things for a woman before you have sex, the more she will push you straight into the friend zone.

It was a wakeup call for Koko when I took my car keys from her. I know it hurts her, but she has been playing me for so fucking long. Cash grass or ass; nobody rides for free. I'm glad I didn't make any problems for her. I wasted too much time chasing her. Now I'm letting her chase me. Or it's really time to move on! I was the backup man; you don't miss your water till your well runs dry. Now I don't feel bad if I start . . . seeing other women! Brother, you only have so much time in life. You better experience as much as you can while you are in the right condition. My mind keeps racing with ideas of ex-lovers. Love is strange. If you really love someone, you don't want to hurt them even if they have hurt you. Koko will think one day on our missed connection. You have to be mature enough not to hurt back and just accept things as they are! But if I am true to myself, I have not been honest with her. She will always be my friend because she helped me when I was down, she was there for me 100 per cent even without giving me sex. This is a fact I must accept and never forget. I would not be human if I said it doesn't hurt. No pain, no gain. Suck it up, Private. Yes, sir!

Dear Koko, I love you, and I always will. I can't ever hurt you because you have been kind and helped me. I know you. I know how you smell, and I see all your weakness. Someday I know you will regret your actions, lies, and mistrust. I was good to you, but you were never true and only acted to be my friend when it comes to love. I'm sorry things didn't work out for us. There are so many things that I let you get away with, but I realize that my age has a lot to do with it.

See the false as false, the true as true.

Survival of the fittest means "the continued existence of." Organisms that are best to adapt to their environment will survive with the extinction of others, as a concept in Darwin's theory of evolution. Now what this means to all you dumb ones is that you must build and master a strong mind and body to compete for a living. Like Bruce Lee, the actor, you must get your mind, body, and soul together! So that means if you are not strong, you will not exist. Master yourself, my young girl or boy.

1. Catch yourself when you start the blame game.
2. Take responsibility.
3. Catch yourself when you're resisting life.

4. Cultivate acceptance and asking, "Okay, now what?"
5. Recognize that difficult circumstances are there to test you.
6. Establish practices that keep you connected.
7. Learn to pay attention to what you need.
8. Learn to overrule your mind.

Mind Shift Required

Life is not about cruising through easy street banking and cash and playing to your heart's content. Difficult stuff happens (shit). Illnesses, accidents, deaths, losses, betrayals, divorces, failures—these will all happen to you at one time or another. What's more important is how you perceive and what you do with it. When the going gets tough, resolve to make it through. When the going gets tough, remind yourself that you can choose to struggle or you can choose to grow. When the going gets tough, celebrate because you're about to get tougher. Defiant, *yes*. But I knew I needed to call on that determined and focused energy from within to get me through this tough time. I had to make a stand. I had to write it down to convince myself. I could do it! And I have. The sun will shine in my life, so there!

Super Bowl

"The winner sows hatred because the loser suffers. Let go of winning and losing and find joy." Football and life are so much alike. Really, you must look and be strong in order to be fit. And that means like they say, in jail you must get paid, and that means work out at least one hour every day to be considered to be in shape. I go to the gym today and work out hard lifting weights and doing leg lifts to help my lower body. The game was everything I guessed it would be. I told my mother "If you give Tom the ball with any time I left on the clock, you would be in trouble." It seemed like a college playoff game or chess playing on the sellevision's stage. The stronger QB wins again and still wanting more. A true Super Bowl in every detail. I can imagine what is life is like at least on the outside. Last summer, I worked on his old home he sold to Dr. Dre for about 20 million and so change. I have the pictures on my phone; I worked with a firm to support the foundation of his home. Shit, it takes him ten minutes to walk from one end of his home to the other side. The BBQ pit looks over the ocean, and I saw Bambi the deer in the woods and a few foxes there also.

How to Compliment a Girl

Compliment a girl for how beautiful she looks, and stare at her often. Compliment her with words. Compliment her skills. Compliment her femininity. Compliment a girl with your chivalry. If you're ever confused about complimenting a girl, some of the best aspects to complimenting are her eyes, her hair, her lips, her fragrance, her voice. Dress really well. Show your confidence. Be a man whom she is proud to be with. Be a man in control of his life. Be that alpha male. Your ego matters. Show her your wit and charm. Don't be a push-over. Work out and look good naked, and be a man who knows how to use his tongue.

Chase Women—I Don't Think So!

I was in my room the other day, and a female knocks on my window in the middle of the night. I opened the door. She jumped the gate. She rushed into the bedroom and took off her clothes. Fat pussy lips! I jumped into action. She has everything you can ask from a sister.

A big ass, nice rack, light-skinned, and the mind was totally gone. But my dick was happy as hell. I've had women give me head lately, but her pussy is the bomb. I should have tagged her the last time she was here, but I lost my focus! I was sucking her breast one by one. Brown sugar for real. I got her motor running when I started JBMF yelling down the Y. When the cunt was wet, I drilled her for twenty-five minutes. She was a bitch in heat, and now I looked back, thinking about these other females I was trying to chase. A cat (pussy) will chase you when you don't chase them. Women love money and sex. And like cats they are picky as hell, and man, they have serious game between their legs. Don't ever act like a friend who doesn't want sex. Make her feel sexually to you. And don't ever act like a friend who isn't interested in sex. Don't tell her that you have feelings for her unless he she is very attracted to you. Try to seduce her mind and whisper in that bitch's ear. Do it over and over.

Don't Be an Extra in a Woman's Life

So today I went on set with a female I've been trying to a make a move on. So I got dressed up as she asked. She got excited because I looked good in my suit. She was showing signs of attraction because she was playing with her hair the whole time. She couldn't help herself. It is a dead giveaway when a women plays with her hair. So I stepped up the game.

I whispered words in French she couldn't understand. Then I made my move when she said she had a good time and she made money. Then she said he she needed space. The exact same words Koko used to speak. So to make a long story short, they are friends to a sisterhood thing and all. So her body says one thing, and she speaks the words every true player hates to hear, "She only wants to be friends," to which I replied, "I don't want to be your friend." I got inside her head for sure. I told her she was a desirable woman, and I know she like it! (Boy.) I told her I would dream about her tonight! Yeah! I'll be that jerk. I rather be known as that than a man who won't make a pass to move her. No way, I'm getting pussy, so the rejection doesn't matter. I don't put none of them above me. As a hardcore man of the world goes about life, I have shown her the door, and I bet the farm she will call me back.

Why? Because I'm being honest. And I not a brother or a friend! But the wonderful thing about Diamond is that she talks to me like we are already married, like my ex-wife to some extent. She is sending mixed signs. I know where I stand for now. Diamond is smart about some things. She is a woman a man could value. She looks good, and she can cook, and if you looked at us, we look like that couple. We both are light-skinned, and she has a mole on the same place you have on your face. Plus I can never forget the facts. She did cook for me. She and Koko help me when I was down. I don't ever forget, but the game forces me to dogish. Be a man. It's a thin line between love and hate. Just be yourself, and horny things will work out. I was so horny trying to come chase a woman, and nature sent one out of the blue to put out the fire.

So if I were a sucker with money, that female would love to take the advantage of an older cat, just because that's how girls are wired. You can't let a hot girl take away from your manhood. Don't place them above you, and don't chase them. Save your money and your time on a female who wants to be with you. Don't push it; don't force it!

So today, I went on set with a female I've been trying to make a move on. I got dressed up suit and tie to make my move. She was showing signs of attraction because she was playing with her hair the whole time we were talking. I whispered words in French she couldn't understand. Then I made my move when she said she had a good time. Wow! Then she said she needed space same exact words Koko used to say. But to make a long story short she says she only want to be friends. And I told her I don't want to be her friend. I got inside her head for sure. I told her she was a desirable woman and I know she like it. (Boy.) I told her I would dream about her tonight! I'm a creep! But I rather be known as a man who makes a pass at them than to be thought of as I was! I'm getting pussy, so the rejection doesn't matter. I showed her the door, and I bet the farm she will call me back for being honest. At least I am not a brother or a friend. But the wonderful thing about Diamond is that she talks to me like we are already married. She used to send me mixed signal, but not now. I know where I stand. She is my friend in so many ways because I can't forget her or Koko helping me when I was down.

It's like we are the exact opposite of each other and I like that at times with her.

Facts Are Reality

In the real world, this is the fact that I must bear in mind. The women I have been spending most of my time with are just friends. In other words, they want you to be their girlfriend. So the action from here is mostly I disappear and not spend any more time with them unless it's about sex. Studies show that there is about 99 percent possibility that sex is not going to happen. So open your mind and accept the facts. So can you master your emotions dealing with females? Stop spending time on females who don't give it up. You are trying way too hard. Everyone talks about Mother Nature, but they forget about Father Time. My son Ricky, twenty-three, now came by the shop today. I repaired the headlight and met his new girlfriend. She was cute, black hair, short, and pretty. Good women are attracted to him now, but he will learn that his education or lack of it will be a problem in his life.

Enter Action with Boldness

"If you are unsure of an action, do not attempt it! Your doubts and hesitations will infect your execution. Timidity is dangerous! Better to enter with boldness. Any mistakes you commit through audacity are easily connected with more audacity. Everyone admires the bold; no one honors the timid. Stand out, make yourself, a magnet of attention by appearing larger, more colorful, more mysterious than the bland and timid masses. Never put too much trust in friends; they will betray you more quickly for they are easily aroused to envy" (Robert Greene, *The 48 Laws of Power*).

My son and his girlfriend spend the day going to the junkyard. Her name is Chantel, or Ruby was her middle name. Small girl, long black hair, and fine Roman-like looks, large eyes like olives, small frame. We didn't find all the parts we searched for, but we did have fun looking. On returning from the junk yard, we changed the damaged hood latch, and change oil was in order. So on the way back from Auto Zone, we stopped and got a good food. Shrimp cooked fresh in the open air. Cooked just like the folks in New Orleans. It was twelve bucks of super taste buds. Every Sunday, all the cool everyday people listen to reggae and smoke mad blunts and dance to the drums. Congo drums were beating, beating soul beats . . . and out of the blue, the Queen Delilia showed up, looking good, her breast looking full and sexy. I didn't chase her; I couldn't any way I because of my leg, so I called out her name, which she quickly answered to. She smiled. I want you to meet my son and his girlfriend. She talked to a woman selling bean pies for a moment, and then she finally got to the area my son was standing. I wondered in the back of my mind did, *Did she just show up, or did she see my car and did some chasing?* And I am guessing that she was doing just that. I was really in my dog mode, and I wanted to chase, but my mind told me to act different from my first idea to run after her even when she disappeared as fast as she got there. She was an exciting looking woman. I would love to have her for a girlfriend, but that window may have already be gone. A queen is a queen!

La La Land

Wow! A super movie. I love it. It's a dream in every way. A dream which may not ever come true. And everyone in LA who is a real actor has deep ties to this film. I have been blessed to have a little part in this Hollywood dream. The love of LA in the film industry. In the park at the observatory, I used to get high with my girlfriend and we spent so many hours. It was our getaway. I used to run the area for miles. For over twenty years, I ran up and down the Hollywood hills. Someone in crowd, is Land better than *Grease*. And that is saying a lot because I love *Grease*, but look out for the newcomer! I love it. I see myself in the male lead with dealing with women and love and dreams. It's a sweet life regardless of the problems and desires. The female emotional side of me cries, but the male side remains silent. My book report, "They worship everything, they value nothing" was a line from the movie I won't forget!

As an actor, this film was in the vein of *Birdman*, which was done a few years back. My bloodline is jazz, so this film is my calling. In a city of stars trying to make dreams come true, boy meets girl. They fall for each other, and at the end of the movie, dreams are fulfilled, but the sad part is that they don't have each other at the end of the movie, kinda like my life with Koko. Always chasing the girl but never getting her in the end. Rats, just like real life. The actors Emma Stone and Ryan Gosling are superb.

Five-star rating from *moi*!

Tips on Being a Real Alpha Male

1. Be real with yourself.
2. Do your thing.
3. Seek to do that which you fear.
4. Live a life of a warrior.
5. Have the courage to fail gloriously.
6. Become self-reliant.
7. Build the body of an alpha male.
8. Get in a fist fight.
9. At some point, stop asking for help.
10. Don't underestimate your internal strength and power.
11. Become a voracious reader!

Ralph Waldo Emerson is an American poet and essayist. A man must be self-reliant physically to take care of himself, where he doesn't need someone to build his house, hunt for our food, fix his cars, or write his reports. We can take care of ourselves and truly forge our own path in life. "The world ain't all sunshine and rainbows." This what I told my son when he texts for help.

It's a very mean and nasty place, this world, and I don't care how tough you are. It will beat you to your knees and keep you there permanently if you let it! It's only through becoming self-reliant that you can ensure that you can take care of yourself and those around you.

Hollywood Recreation Center (1986)

All the ballers, the street ballers, the best in town, came to the Hollywood Recreation Center. All the music people and actors, stand-up comics like Robin Harris would play serious street ball and talk plenty of smack. They played the dozens, which means talk about your momma!

Some brothers took it to heart and wanted to fight Robin. Robin kept a gun in his car, but he never let things get out of hand.

ROBIN: I'm going to do a movie with Spike Lee. It'd called *Do the Right Thing, Muhammad.* You, yeah right. Tell me anything, I was born yesterday. Fool Robin? Fuck you, man! I bet your real name ain't Muhammad. What is your real slave name? Your mama didn't call you that name, nigger!

MUHAMMAD: My name was Richard Leon Brown Jr.

ROBIN: Ain't that about a bitch? I bet you want a pork chop sandwich right now.

The park drew all sorts of black folks and everyone else who wanted to show off skills. Dmack was the star in those days. He had the best all-around game. He was quick. He played defensive and attacked with his quickness. I always was in his face, and we battled many a game. Shooting was not my game. I loved to play tight defense on anyone. Eddie was from Chicago, and he and Robin would go back and forth seeing who could talk them and trash and score the most points. The singer Rick James would come out to give it to you, baby! That sweet and funky stuff. There were professional ball players that played; one was Lou Brown.

Lou Brown played for UNLV running rebels. He played against the best in the world and played for Italian team and wore the best suit in the world, but he ended smoking drugs and dying homeless at some street corner in Hollywood. A great talent gone to the curb. And the star of the park on the sellevision show was Terry Knox, a cool white cat who had the TV show about it, the war. *Tour of Duty*—it was the only show where veterans would get paid more just for playing veterans because they knew how to march, salute, handle a weapon, wear the correct uniform and medals. And there was the captain, Nelson Pigford, who wrote for Barry White and sang in *Rocky 2*. He was about six-six. And there was Chris and Slim. They were the first men who were not scared to be gay. Slim was tall, and Chris was small. Both could rock the ball. Rob was a singer. He came from Motown, DC. He had skills. Kevin too. Cowboy and green eyes, had shooting wars, which all enjoyed. Big Mike played semi-pro. We used to call him Fall Back because when he shot the ball, it was automatic fall back. Donoto Baker, who was bigger than Mike Tyson. KV, a rapper who is Snoop Dog's cousin, and sang on Tupac album *All Eyez on Me* record. Dollar Bill, a rapper from New Orleans. Big Game James, Perkins, Chi, the Fox Brothers, Carlos, Dave, Cassius, Lefty, Slow Mo, Gorilla, Norman Carter, Don, CQ, and the rest of the cast LC. Mark the Chills Wills was a boxer I trained with my great footwork. I was the rabbit running miles like it ain't shit.

Kelly, who was a gang member, broke my jaw at the park for getting a ticket on his car. I was going to kill him for attacking me when my back was turned. Lucky for me, an older Jewish man talked me out of it. He said, "If you kill him, you will be throwing your life away." Thank God, I didn't pull the trigger on that shotgun that day, or I would not be writing this book from home but from jail. He was a bully by his size, and a smaller man shot him in the back, and now Kelly is in a wheelchair, and he tried to sell drugs from his chair only to go back to the penitentiary. He and Ron and Dave and Chicago would go in and out of the evil system. Kelly may not ever see sunlight on the outside, and that was the life wanted by him for him! I did understand gang members, just seems like wasted reasons to act a damn fool. I'm glad I listened to the wise old man; he saved my life. So Robin Harris and the crew would play ball and talk shit for hours. They played ball, drank beer, and when it got dark, they would play craps until the police threw them out the park. Big Jeff had been to the penitentiary, and he was big and strong. He kicked ass and took names—Prince, Spider, Tom, Randal, Pretty Tony, Bill, Sunny, Ralph, Nate, Jay, Scotty (Terry's driver).

Oscars 2017

Tannya is a must-see movie. I worked the Oscars way back in 2005. My post was in front of the Chinese Man Theater. My job was to look at everyone's passes to enter the red carpet and the awards show. On every pass, there is a symbol that had to be seen with the naked eye. After everyone was inside, my next location was the Governor's Ball. That is where all the action is, where all the stars eat their food.

It's also a place where actors get the hot deals with the industry managers, agents, publicist, etc. The Goodyear Blimb was buzzing overhead the whole time. It feels great helping protect so many important people.

The Jimi and Matt fight was a great act! *Lion* is a movie I must see also. The award show started with an African- American winning Jimmy made a joke about OJ getting and extra slice of meat for his sandwich! Wow! Violia's speech was superb. Very emotional, which feels good. I had a chance to work with her on *How to Get Away with Murder*. *La La Land* wins, no big surprise. Fame was great for black actors this year.

A surprise ending for *La La Land* being beaten for best picture by *Moonlight*! *Hell or High Water* is a must-see film.

Shining Star

"When you wish upon a star, your dreams will take you very far. But when you wish upon a dream, life ain't always what it seems. What'd you see on a night so clear, in the sky so very dear. You're a shining star no matter who you are. Shining bright to see. What you could truly be (what you could truly be), shining star come into view. Shine its watchful light on you. Give you strength to carry on. Make your body big and strong. Born a man child of the sun. Saw my work had just begun. Found I had to stand alone. Bless it now I've got my own. So if you find yourself in need, why don't you listen to these words of heed? Be a giant grain of sand. Words of wisdom, yes, I can. You're a shining star. No matter who you are. Shining bring to see what your life can truly be. Shining star for you to see, what your life can truly be" (Earth, Wind & Fire).

So I met her at her home, finally getting major hunger pangs at this point. She hopped in the driver's seat of the car, and we drove to King's Buffet and started to chow down on some good food. She asked me a lot of questions, but she had no idea that it was her lucky day. I finally had to realize that if my son is turning twenty-four today, it's time for me to man up and give Koko my total commitment. I know she may not make me happy. She had so many problems in her own life. I wanted a girl who by nature was like my mother, so we shall see what happens next. We go to Norman's show, fifty bucks. And man, you know the music is great, and she has never heard these songs. I sang them in her ears, so she will always remember my words! Super event. It was a perfect day. We didn't have sex, her bad. I have to wait for her to grow up. She is very, very slow. But I want her in my life regardless. I've got her complete attention. Norman turned out to be the greatest wing man a friend could ask for. The best love song of my time.

So I wrote Koko and told her I want to be the main man in her life. And we will be friends, and I will always love her. Sounds emotional, but that's what makes bestsellers. I don't want to harm a fly; I'm in the mood for love!

March 4, 2017

Wake up! I thought it would be a normal day; it was not by a long shot. I went to the gas station. It was my son's birthday. My mother had sent about $20. I added another $40. He and his girlfriend, I gave them a ride back to their home. They planned to eat BBQ, and out of the blue, after twenty-two days—and I counted each day on my chalkboard like I were in jail—the one and only Koko calls me! I'm excited. "Let's go to King's Buffet for dinner." Wow! The female mind. Anyway, getting back to working the shop. A singer named Jerry was getting his oil changed when he told me a friend I've been knowing for years Norman Carter pulled up to Mobil. Cool! Norman told me of a spot tonight he would be singing. I've had been out on the road with him, and I know all the songs he sings almost by heart. So my plan to buy a ring for Koko. Go home, shower, and get dressed. Wait around for an hour for the ring to be fitted to her size. So she called as I walked my slow ass back to pick up the fitted ring.

La La
Many guys have come to you
With a line that wasn't true
And you passed them by (passed them by)
Now you're in the center ring
And their lines don't mean a thing
Why don't you let me try (let me try)
Now I don't wear a diamond ring
I don't even have a song to sing
All I know is
La la la la la la la la la means
I Love you
Oh, baby please now
Oh, baby

La la la la la la la la la means
I love you
If I ever saw a girl
That I needed in this world
You are the one for me (one for Me)
Let me hold me in my arms
Girl, and thrill you with my charms
I'm sure you will see (you will see)
The things I am saying are true
And the way I explain them to you, yes to you
Listen to me
Coda (repeat to fade):
La la la la la la la la la means
(1: Oh, you'll have to understand
Come on and take my hand)
(Thomas Randolph Bell,
William Alexander Hart)

Audition
My aunt to live in Paris
I remember she used to
come home and tell us
these stories about being
abroad and I remember
she told us that she
jumped into the river once
barefoot
She smiled
Leapt without looking, and
tumbled into the Seine
The water was freezing
She spent a month sneezing
But said she would do it again.
Here's to the ones who dream
Foolish as they may seem.
Here's to the heart's that ache

Here's to the mess we make.
She captured a feeling
Shy with no ceiling
The sunset inside a frame.
She lived in her liquor and died with a flicker,
I'll always remember the flame.
Here's to the one who dream
Foolish as they may seem
Here's to the ones who dream
Foolish as they may seem
Here's to the hearts that ache,
Here's to the mess we make
She told me
A bit of madness is key
To give us new colors to see
Who know where it will lead us?
And that why they need us.
So bring on the rebels,
The ripples from pebbles
The painters and poets and plays
And here's to the fools who dream
Crazy as they may seem.
Here's to the mess we make.
I trace it all back to then.
Her and the snow, and the Seine
Smiling through it
She said she'd do it again
(Justin Hurwitz, Benj Pasek, Justin
Noble Paul, Emma Stone)

Wisdom
Wise people are not absorbed
in their own needs.
They take the needs of all people as their own.
They are good to the good.
But they are also good to those

who are still absorbed in their own needs.
Why?
Because goodness is in the very nature
of the Great Integrity.
Wise people trust
those who trust.
But they also trust those who do not trust.
Why?
Because trusting is in the very nature
Of the Great Integrity.
Wise people merge with all others
rather than stand apart judgmentally.
In this way, all begin to open
their ears and hearts.
More prepared to return to the
innocence of childhood.
(Lao Tzu, Tao Te Ching)

The Real Competitor

"The real competitor is the one who gives all he has all the time" (Bruce Lee). Never give up! The one key to success with women: "Have no fear for the future: the future is ours" (Louis Farrakhan).

It's time for self-determination. It is rare these days to have a man speaks for the weak against the powers that be. It takes a real man to do that! I was blessed to get some understanding from the nation. I looked back when I was young and black and proud and mad as hell as how they killed anyone who stood up to the power elite.

We were blessed to have great role models. Muhammad Ali was a brave man. I'm glad our worlds crossed. I miss him and love him. When we prayed together, the speaker said that Allah (God) loves the great and the small. We are all brothers no matter what place you have in the world. We feel sorry for today's kids. They look up to all kinds of kooks and weirdoes.

The most honorable Elijah Muhammad said we want freedom and we want justice, which is what all people want. His slave name was Pool! And what he did was he pooled black folks' money and built black-owned hospitals, banks farmers, etc. And the *Muhammad Speaks* newspaper is everywhere in America. I used to fry the wholesome fish and make the fresh bean pies. I would later cook pies, cookies, cakes on a large super scale in the core, but at that time, my Sharon was down for me regardless of the fact that I couldn't pay my bills and give my labor to the nation. After he died (may the peace and blessing be with him), I entered the war, which was badboy training, with real warriors fighting weapons. I see real weakness without weapons, but the Buddha in me is still for nonviolence because my soul tells me that is the real victory. The real victory is against your own ego, mind, and soul. The master conquers himself. That is the best prize.

"The whole history of humankind is basically the definition of who is us and who is them and the question of whether we should all live under the same set of rules. We are programmed biologically instinctively to prefer win-lose situations, us versus them. We have to find a way to bring simple, personal decency and trust back to our politics" (Bill Clinton).

Bad boys think for themselves. Bad boys aren't followers. Bad boys don't flinch.

"Jeet Kune Do is the art not founded on techniques or doctrine. It is just as you are" (Master Bruce Lee). Believe in yourself! "Have faith in your abilities! Without humble but reasonable confidence in your own powers you cannot be successful or happy. But with sound self-confidence you can succeed. A sense of inferiority and inadequacy interferes with the attainment of your hopes, but self-confidence leads to self-realization and successful achievement. Because of the importance of this mental attitude, this book will help you believe in yourself and release your inner powers" (Norman Vincent Peale, *The Power of Positive Thinking*). "Who decides whether you shall be happy or unhappy? The answer—you do!"

Malcolm X

Malcom X's original slave name is Malcolm Little, a.k.a. Al Hajj Malik Shabazz. He is a very wise man. I've seen films and movies about him. He was an outstanding man. "If you are not an angry black man in America, you are an insane black man in America."

"When my mother was pregnant with me, she told me later, a party of hooded Ku Klux Klan riders galloped up to our home in Omaha, Nebraska, one night. Surrounding the house, brandishing their shot guns and rifles, they shouted for my father to come out. My mother went to the front door and opened it. Standing where they could see her pregnant condition, she told them that she was alone with her three small children that she was alone with her three small children and that my father was away, preaching in Milwaukee. The Klansmen shouted threats and warning at her that we had better get out of town because the good Christian white people, were not going to stand for my father 'spreading trouble' among the good Negroes of Omaha with the 'back to Africa' preaching of Marcus Garvey."

"I don't have a degree like many of you out there before me have. But history don't care anything about your degrees. The white man, he has filled you with fear of him from ever since you were little black babies. So over you is the greatest enemy a man can have, and that is fear. I know some of you are afraid to listen to the truth you have been raised on fear and lies. But I am going to preach to you the truth until you are free of the fear. Your slavemaster, he brought you over here, and of your past everything was destroyed. Today, you do not know your true language. What tribe are you from? You would not recognize your tribe's name if you heard it. You don't know nothing about your true culture. You don't even know your family's real name. You are wearing a white man's name! The white slave master, who hates you. You are a people who think you know all about the bible and all about Christianity you even foolish enough to believe that nothing is right but Christianity. You are the planet Earth's only group of people ignorant of yourself, ignorant of your own kind, of your true history/ignorant of your enemy!"

"You know nothing at all but what your white slave master has chosen to tell you. And he has told you only that will benefit himself, and his own kind. He has taught you for his benefit, that you are a neutral, shiftless, helpless so called 'Negro.' I say so-called because you are not a negro. There is no such thing as a race of negroes."

"Out of the huts of history's shame, I rise up from the past that's rooted in pain. I rise" ("Rise," Maya Angelou).

"It's important to know the stuff you came from" ("The Stuff," Afeni Shakur).

An old man was asked, "What is the secret of happiness?"
The old man said, "I haven't any great secret. It's just as plain as the nose on your face. When I get up in the morning, I have two choices—either to be happy or to be unhappy. And what do you think I do? I just choose to be happy, and that's all there is to it."

Birth of a Nation

Is this film the reason why only a few black actors get work today? A white woman jumps to her death rather then get raped by a black man. A powerful message to white folks that black men are wild and crazy people. So they can lock you up and make you a slave. Intellectual warfare is needed for black folks so we can break the chains of slavery. We must act on the idea that we can win for ourselves and our loved ones.

"No one in white America understands what black men go thru in America." Someone in the government spoke these profound words.

The great Tiger Woods says that he learned from his father that talking to his kids eye to eye on the same level makes a great bond with the kids. Wise words of advice. He has kids and someday grandkids. Our future must show reflection of the life we live as black folks. We must talk to our kids about how to act around the police so they don't go out into the world not knowing what might happen and how to be alive after you encounter the police in a car or in the street. Even as a grown man, you can be a target for police abuse.

"The slave went free, stood a brief moment in the sun, then moved back again toward slavery" (W. E. B. Dubois).

Most movies, movements, and ideas keep repeating this thought in American history, then and now on all levels of our community. The magnanimity of the birth of a nation is the hard facts in white America still today, but the world sees it now.

Art as Propaganda

The height of art's symbolic power, of course, has been used as propaganda to convey a political message. It remains the foundation of the advertising industry, which exists solely to cajole and manipulate. This film was a tool used by the existing power base to reinforce its key messages. This film was made in the Jim Crow era, so black people were treated as less than zero and still are in many ways. America is blowing smoke up black folks' asses, but it's time for us to wake up and come together.

Angela Davis for President

Davis opposed the 1995 Million Man March, arguing that the exclusion of women from this event necessarily promoted male chauvinism. She said that Louis Farrakhan and other organizers appeared to prefer that women take subordinate roles in society. Back in the day, she felt the same about the men in the Black Panthers organization. She is the sexy, super-smart sister who many young women today have never heard of because they have no knowledge of black history, or other women who were down for the people. I love her. In my mind, she is the perfect black women.

In 1967, Davis began public-speaking engagements. She expressed her opposition to the Vietnam War, racism, sexism, and the prison-industrial complex, and her support of gay rights and other social justice movements. She blamed imperialism for the troubles suffered by oppressed populations.

"We are facing a common enemy and that enemy is Yankee Imperialism, which is killing us, both here and abroad. Now I think anyone who would try to separate those struggles, who would say that in order to consolidate an anti- war movement we have to leave all of these other outlying issues out of the picture, is playing right into the hands of the enemy," she declared.

I am a Black Revolutionary Woman

"The new doctrine was not one of preemptive war which arguably falls within same stretched interpretation of the UN Charter, but rather a doctrine doesn't begin to have any grounds in international law, namely, preventive war. That is, the United States will rule the world by force, and if true is any challenge to its domination whether it is perceived in the distance invented, imagined or whatever-then the United States will have the right to destroy that challenge before it becomes a threat. That preventive war, not preemptive war."

The whole educational system and the whole media system have the opposite goal. You've taught to be a passive, obedient follower. You've likely to be a victim of propaganda, but you have to be willing to develop an attitude of critical examination toward whatever is presented to you. How do you break out of this? Just use your ordinary intelligence. There are no special techniques. Just be willing to examine what's presented to you with ordinary common sense, skeptical intelligence. The United States must be the only country in the world where someone can be called a terrorist for defending his own country from attack.

War Is Peace, Freedom Is Slavery, Ignorance Is Strength (Noam Chomsky)

Democracy is different. It refers to a system in which decisions are made by sectors of the business community and related elites. The public are to be only "spectators of action," not participants. They are permitted to ratify the decisions of their betters and to lend support to one or another of them, but not to interfere with matters like public policy that are none of their business.

Eisenhower says that to keep the Latin Americans in line, you have to put them a little bit and make them think that you make them think that you are fond of them.

"Given all that, US policies in the Third World are easy to understand. We've consistently opposed democracy if its results can't be controlled. The problem with real democracies is that they are likely to fall prey to the heresy that governments should respond to the needs of their own population, instead of those of US investors.

"Some people think that we are racist, because the news media finds it useful to create that impression in order to support the power structure, which we have nothing to do with . . . They like for the Black Panther Party to be made to look like a racist organization, because that camouflages, the true class nature of the struggle. But they find it harder and harder to keep up that camouflage and are driven to campaigns of harassment and violence to try to eliminate the Black Panther Party" (Minister of Defense, Huey P. Newton).

The United States versus Karma

I think sometimes we must go back to find the facts to correct them as a people or a group of peoples. The US has always had a deep dark relationship with all types of men and women. In the science of humans, karma has to be a factor somewhere. All the evil that has been done must have an effect on something, if you believe in God. Many people think the super mind doesn't exist. The jury is still out. In the meantime, I'm trying to not be like Mr. Williams (a.k.a. Jim Kelly) in the movie *Enter the Dragon* when his mate told him, "You better keep your eye on the referee, if you know what I mean." Of course he fights to his death.

White folks have always been afraid of some black man who would rise up and help his people overcome to freedom. They are afraid of the black Halley's Comet on its return to our earth with it spiritual force upon mankind.

Human life is much richer than the conscious human life. Creativity is a disciplined eye. James Brown called it the big payback to all those people who did him wrong. I am going to give this book feedback on the black power book I'm reading. Notes to be posted soon.

"Know this, O good man, that evil things are uncontrollable. Let not greed and wickedness drag you to suffering for a longtime."

"Hard to restrain, unstable is this mind, it flips wherever it lists. Good it is to control the mind. A controlled mind brings happiness."

In our lives, we have two things going on—things our minds remember and things we can't remember. In the course of your life, you will have a great number of experiences which you receive consciously and unite with your ego. So our life is really divided into two parts into a realm of we have never brought really into clear consciousness.

1967: The Summer of Love

Where all the folks of my generation came to the bay area for a Love Inn. My family just came back from the United Kingdom. It was one hundred degrees some days where we were. I got my first taste of hot pussy. We broke blood inside my sleeping bag after going to her home in the middle of the night, slipping in her window at night, wanting more of my goddess with blond pussy hair in my teeth, blossom blouse in full view. First love. Her dad would have killed me if he found us in her room. *Explosive, beautiful,* and *delicate* are some of the words that come to mind. "You're My brown-eyed Girl" came out on the radio in my mind, making love in the green grass, wherever. Life is grand to be young, gifted, and black, walking everywhere in cut-offs, no tops, or riding bikes around our small town near an air force base. My brother Bob and I would both ride go-carts and get burned by hot exhaust pipes.

You don't want to lose your mojo when dealing with all the different kinds of females that were around and who wanted to be with you. The good thing about Sacramento is that if get bored, you can always go to Reno, Nevada, to gamble, play a game for stakes and my cynosure to see all the legal whores. As a young man, this would be heaven on earth. There were super evergreen trees three hundred to five hundred feet as far as the eye could see. One winter almost froze my balls off while I was removing snow from the roof in a small town called Portola, California, with about two hundred folks high in the hills after getting off a roof of snow and having to sleep in a car all night, not fun at all.

I can only remember one cooler night. That all happened chasing some tail. My sweet mother warned me not to go out that night, but no! My dumb ass was thinking with the little head and not his head that everyone sees. Oh, she was so wise. My dumb ass didn't find the girl and had to return home about 3:00 a.m., which pissed her off, but she did let me return. Thanks, Mother dear. I felt so dumb and cold.

The white boy next door was a biker and used to ride with the Hell's Angels. Out of his mind, he used to have wild sex parties in his carport. He would get high on anything pot, meth. He shot wine into his arm, glue, etc. As a young man not knowing about sex, you guess that all white guys have small dicks, but he had a big dick for a white guy, and the fact that I am black, he was trying to show that he was just as much man as me. Whatever, brother. I know he had guns because that's what's up for the gang life. I thought at that time that gangs were to guard the Rolling Stones, and someone got shot and messed up the whole peace vibes. Will the summer of love ever return? No!

Notes from the Dark Side

It is about black people taking care of business—the business of and for black people. One must start from premises rooted in truth and reality rather than myth. Black people in America have no time to play nice, polite parlor games, especially when the lives of their children are at stake.

Never forget three types of people: those who helped you in difficult times, those who left you in difficult times, and those who put you in difficult times.

We all should stop playing the games! White people will always want things to be fine and peaceful. Racism is both overt and convert.

"The dark ghettos are social, political, educational, and above all- economic colonies. Their inhabitants are subject peoples, victims of greed, cruelty, insensitivity, guilt, and fear of their masters" (Dr. Kenneth B. Clark).

Black people are not in a depressed condition because of some defects in their character. The colonial power structure clamped a boot of oppression on the neck of the black people and then ironically said, "They are not ready for freedom."

The Hudson Theatre

As a homeless veteran who used to sleep in his car for about three years, the Hudson Theatre was the place I would use my computer to get work and meet different people and actors my favorite.

I've seen many good plays here and musical numbers. The main person that makes this place great is an actor named Tiffany Thomas. Whatever play or project she is involved in turns out to be a winner. She is so smart and pretty. I used to work on her car from time to time. She is a positive force. The Hudson has three stages, and the cafe is where pictures of giant bulls hang on the walls. Robert, a teacher of acting, played the role of press when Ice Cube checked him in the NWA movie. Nice chap, but expensive.

There was one show, much loved, about a black man who back in the day opened up a record store in the black community, got whites to buy records before the police start getting up tight about it. But they won't let a black man rent a store in Hollywood. Land of the free?

The point is obvious; black people must lead and run their organizations. Black people must bargain from a position of strength, consolidate to be effective.

The Revolution Will Not Be Televised

The goal of the racists is to keep black people on the bottom, arbitrarily and dictatorially, as they have done for over three hundred years. The goal of blacks is self-determination and self-identification! White people must be made to understand that they must stop messing with black people or the blacks will fight back. Dr. Martin Luther King stated clearly that protest marches were not the cause of the racism but merely exposed a long cancerous condition in the society.

White America is super rich, strong, capable of grand designs to conquer space and other scientific feats, but it is woefully underdeveloped in its human and political relations. In these areas, it is primitive and backward!

Black people are saying, "Mr. Charlie, we'd rather do it ourselves. It is only mass struggle that advances us, and only when the masses advance do we advance."

The African struggle in America is part and parcel of the African Revolution. The greatest obstacle to accepting revolution is the shedding of blood. We hear the Pan Africanist Malcolm X saying, "Revolution is bloody. It knows no compromise. It overturns and destroys everything in its path." Our obstacle is lack of mass conscious political organization.

> Alas for the man
> Who raises his hand against another
> And even more for him
> Who returns the blow
> HE never returns evil for evil
> Beware of the anger of the mind
> Master your thoughts
> Let them serve truth
> Freedom

"You get your freedom by letting your enemy know that you'll do anything to get your freedom: then you'll get it. It's the only way you'll get it."

"I'm not going to sit at your table and watch you eat, with nothing on my plate, and call myself a diner . . . Being here in America doesn't make you an American" (Malcolm X).

Wedding in June Rocky Mountain High

I have some very interesting things going on now. I'm starting to see more pictures of my grandson, my son, and friends are starting to pick up, with the wedding date set. And I can't wait to see the adventure begin in June 17. I'm not going to be sad if Koko doesn't come. She still might be playing the little bitch role by then. I'm not chasing her anymore. We have gone as far as we can go. And she decides to go her own way, it might hurt me, but I'm strong to survive. It will be her loss in the long run. But I can't blame Koko. I blame myself, and it's good to always remember that Bob and she helped me when I was in a leg cast and might have fallen backward down the stairs. But no way Koko had your back 100 percent. She may not ever have sex with me, but I will never forget who was there when the times were difficult, to say the least. That was the second time she helped. The first was when she invited me into her home, got me out of the car. Who else but her. So there is a foundation for love.

Even if it is not sexual. I got her the ring because I realize how time is flying, and it has been almost three years since my beloved passed away. Her love was intense after years. Koko is a more educated lady, which is what I need to help me grow. Time is something that can't be wasted. She had never been married, and maybe today's women like to be single, even as the pressure of Father Time is making their child-bearing years pushing in overdrive. She played a key role to my recovery. I yelled at her, tried to piss her off. I'm sure she won't forget my remarks, but I was in so much pain, and I said it anyway, bad things. But her calling a month later proved to be a good thing. If I died tomorrow, I have showed her that I am thankful for her kind words and actions. We know that we will never forget each other as long as we both live.

"Long-term consistency trumps short-term intensity" (Bruce Lee).

Sometimes standing back and remembering that it's about the journey is the perfect protection against the sweating the small stuff. Strive to be positive. You'll find a fair wind and following seas.

Completeness can seem incomplete.

Pornography Problems

"There is no such thing as a moral or an immoral book," said Oscar Wilde. "Books are well written or badly written. That is all." Not much has changed in a hundred years! Since then, Congress established and funded a National Commission on Pornography. Its report that was published in 1970, the year I got out of high school, found that it was not pornography but the puritanical attitudes toward pornography that cause problem in America.

Pornography doesn't degrade women. Women are degraded by our culture. We have a serious problem with the way women are treated in our culture, and pornography is a symptom. Pornography should not be censored. Censorship applies basically to these subjects: sex, violence, and ideas. Censorship of ideas is by far the most serious. It is also by far the most subtle.

Our popular culture has gone far beyond propagandizing for fornication. That seems almost innocent nowadays. What America increasing produces and distributes is now propaganda for every perversion and obscenity imaginable.

Politicians and Free Speech

It all boils down to this. Nobody in this country or anywhere else has any inalienable rights, not the right to free speech or freedom of religion or assembly, not the right to keep and bear arms, not the right to be free from unreasonable searches and seizures.

There always will be scoundrels who will try to take away your rights if they believe they can get away with it. And there always will be fools who will let them do it. The only rights that we have, the only rights that we can depend on are those that we are willing and able to fight for, to shed blood for. And that's what's coming to in this country very soon.

Censorship is also crucial to protect children and the rest of us from men encouraged to act by a steady diet of computerized pedophilia, murder, rape, and sadomasochism.

Mariah in Los Angeles, City of Angels

Well, Friday on Facebook I learned that my grandchild Mariah is in town. She just posted that she is at the LA Zoo. Wow! I'm excited, but I have to wait until Sunday before I met up with her and Ricky. I try to reach Koko, but she is not on the radar. That sucks. I'm thinking that she is on the rag or crabby about something.

I still must test myself not to explore with emotions when it comes to the opposite sex. It's hard to control my emotions at times. But being an older man, I must learn to wait. I keep violating the wisdom and laws that break karma's laws; I keep making mistakes. I let my guard down to some weak people since I lost my friend three years ago. It's hard to forget fifteen years with a woman. I keep on chasing her. She goes up and down, in and out of my life. I keep loving her countless times, and her mind. She knew me more than anyone living. She was wild and a rebel and very pretty. She had wonderful hair and lips. She was sweet, taboo, dangerous, and sexy. She was so kind to animals, and she never changed to please anyone. Relaxation to a past that can't return. Move on! That an order! Left, right, left. The women of today are not the same breed as the women of yesterday. It is what it is; the real master wants nothing.

A master gives up mischief. Very hard to do! Bad news, the writer's strike starts talks tomorrow, and the strike will start on the 18th. I'm not working now, so a strike won't affect my income, which has been zero. And I don't know, is it an age factor or with all the anti-Muslim in America that they are not taking any chances hiring us? It's a hard place to be at this point in my life. But I can't give up! I had two films come out this year. Both with high rating. So I'm happy, and my new goal is to walk slowly and then faster, the running again! It's a cruel world, with or without women! Outwit the desire to hurt. Your loved ones can cause the most pain because they know your weakness. My ego has to learn to adjust at a certain point. I must remain focused and not let females derail my mission in life. They are really weak; they won't last ten minutes in the Marine Corps. One day of PT would kill them. They would cry home to their mommies and daddies. They would breakdown within two minutes with a DI. The real DI would crew them up like rag dolls. He would show them how weak and lazy they really are with their lives. Motivation and determination is the key to winning, and staying strong is the best move in this stage of life. I must keep my mind on the training I learned from the master.

Good Day

A star is born, and her name is Mariah Brown. She has landed in Los Angeles, Friday. I saw her on Facebook, standing at the Beverly Hills, with the sign in the background. Sunday morning, after waiting for contact by phone, she went to Long Beach to see the aquarium of the Pacific! She and her girlfriend made their way toward us. I saw my beautiful grandchild, and we met with my handsome son Ricky and his girlfriend. I got her some black hand soap from an African brother whom I see weekly. I gave her some money so she could shop at the mall.

While she and her best friend went to the mall, Ricky and his girl and his friends came over and watched a 007 movie and smoked some buds. We talked about the different places, Seattle and the northwest versus Los Angeles. I got up early on Monday, and we met at Denney's by the airport, and I gave her mom's address and some movies to take home to her mother. She leaves today at noon. She says she wants to return to see San Diego in July. I'm happy she finally came down. So I know that our lives will be united. I will help her with her life, and I know that she loves me like my sisters loved my grandfather, so now I know what it feels like. This is why our lives came together, and I know in my soul I will be a positive force in her life. Today, my mother said that when family get together, "it's a good day." Mariah asked me some good questions about my past, like the whereabouts of Rich's mothers, which drew a blank! I know now that she wants to come back and live here and open the window of serendipity.

The movie connection. I gave Mariah a movie updated *King Kong*, which was okay! But the connection is that the first movie I ever saw in a theater was *King Kong*, and I remember my grandfather picking us up in San Vincent DePaul trucks. We all sat in the front seat of the cab. The man always gave us food, toys, and love. I hated his fake teeth sitting in a glass in the bathroom. But I love the man who spoke with a real soft but gracious voice. I saw him break a chicken's neck and let it run around the backyard. Guess what's for dinner, with gravy and all the fixing, washed down with sweet-ened lemonade. Damn, we forgot about that bird after a while but never the lessons. He showed hard work and strong family values. He loved to tell jokes and have fun with his family. We called him the Godfather on a James Brown tip. He loved his wife and kids!

"You gave up your life when you gave birth," a wise woman once said. "There are only rebels and tyrants now" (XXX). So much has happened since I have written anything. A black man was killed by himself after killing a man in cold blood. Sad! And later that day, a black man, whose name is Muhammad, killed four humans, three because they were white. Another person used violence to kill with-out reason. These are senseless acts. Men lose with unclear thinking, wanting to hurt and not help the human family.

And then I got a surprise phone call from my father. We talked shortly. He seemed like he was in good spirits. He told me that he lost his right leg and he has not seen his sister Amy in a while and that age and time has slowed down her mind. She repeats herself. He is waiting to get his leg soon, which I could tell made him happy! Good. In my mind, I didn't want to baby him. I'm glad he reached out!

My mother asked me for Mariah's phone number, which is great. I want them to stay connected because that's my granddaugh-ter, my female offspring. "Truth is powerful, and it prevails." These are words spoken by my mother in another time and place.

Sojourner Truth

"It is not the strongest of the species that survives, nor the most intelligent factor survives. It is the one that is the most adaptable to change" (Charles Darwin).

The master Bruce Lee would have loved this message, but even he in his films would say that every style has an inherent weakness. He would just say be fast and quick. The Marine training I got was very proactive, meaning that your body never forgets the training. The same goes for the mind. After my father lost his leg, his father lost an arm, if I do recall. So as I get older, I must follow the master's lessons even if he has been gone for years. He died the same year as my grandmother, bless her heart. I did pay my respect to teach the last time I was in Seattle with my son and grandchild. I must learn from my father's mistakes as far as food is concerned. Stay away from rich foods. That is a serious issue when it comes to the male side of my bloodline. Bruce would just say be like water!

Charles Darwin was an English naturalist, geologist and biologist who wrote *On the Origin of Species*, which is about natural selection, in which the struggle for existence involves in selective breeding, and *The Descent of Man, and Selection in Relation to Sex*.

Koko and Facebook

After weeks of silence from Koko, she appeared on Facebook with her girlfriend who just got married, Meme. They looked like they were having big fun at the beach. So I "liked" the photo and made a statement like, "Who is your girlfriend? She's kind of cute." Sunday rolled around, and I was going to the gym after watching the playoff games on ABC. Koko called me at 7-eleven. I was surprised, but I had a feeling she might call. I was happy and excited. We met up at Sunset + Vine. We hugged and drove away. We were looking for something to eat. I was going to eat meat, but she wanted something green. So I went to the Hudson Theatre and grabbed some good meals to go. I kept driving down Santa Monica west, past Beverly Hills, and I told her about seeing Mariah on Facebook in front of the sign. We turned right on Ocean, toward Malibu. We looked at the American Dream and wanted a part of it. She wanted to use the restroom at some fast-food place. We went down the street to an RV campsite, where I got a fifty-dollar ticket for parking violation. We ate our food on the rocks and watched the waves hit the shoreline. She just got back in town, and I asked her where the ring I got her. She said she left it at home and she didn't want to lose it. I was kind of hurt, seeing a mood ring, but I tried not to show my feeling. I could tell that she was still not into me sexually, but I have a chance, if I will have to take my time. If I even have a real shot. She said she wanted to go to the alley to look for some dresses this weekend; we would see.

Well, today is *La La Land* in Los Angeles, the love letter film of this town. The movie has so many places and things done over the years. I love this movie. Koko and I stopped back in Hollywood to pick up some ice cream, and I drove her back to her place. She said she was tired from the trip. I told her about the wedding in June, and she can come, but that depends on her job. I understand, and I put it out there any way. I have three women born under the same sign, each one very different, but all love family. Anyway, I have planted the seed of love with the giving of the ring, so like *La La Land*, we will see if the guy gets the girl in the end, or is it just a wild ride about a dream that does not come true?

We have to make a song from the heart and cry tears of joy for living a wonderful life as it is, trying to make a better way. Higher states of mind, peace of mind in your soul. The ways of the world make the heart grow cold, but love conquers all in the world and beyond the stars. It comes into view when it is all said and done.

May Day 2017

Labor workers from all over the world will take Monday off to strike and show support for all workers. May Day in the past has meant bloodshed and revolution in Russia and elsewhere. *Mayday* is the sign of the call when an airplane is in distress. The word *strike* will be seen on Monday for sure. Back in the day before Ken Howard, SAG would hold a Labor Day picnic for all the membership. I won a phone at one, lucky me. But that was then. Now they don't want to spend money on it, only Christmas party affairs, which show weakness with other unions.

May Day was also the day shit started with Rodney King, who was beaten by four white cops almost to death. It's tough being a black man in America.

My son was inside his mother during the riots. "We got pampers and liquor," said Ricky's mother, and her male friend came back from the Korean supermarket that was looted. I remember seeing Korean men on the top of their business with guns firing their weapons at folks, driving past, putting on the gas to exit the area. Cops were scared as fuck. They were riding four deep, not stopping for nothing. Then the real shit happened. While I was driving my old Chevy wagon town car, a telephone pole that was on fire almost fell down, hitting the hood. Wires were on fire; sparks were everywhere. One the first day of the riots, I was working on a TV show called *Man versus Machine*. A show about a female robot cop. I had a cop uniform on. As we watched on the TV set, the whole city began to burn. About time I returned to the hood, I saw stores burning, the fish burning, glass everywhere, burned down! Oh no! Then I saw gang members with guns and cars with all kinds of stuff. The local gun store was robbed. I remember saying to myself, *My mother didn't raise a thief. If I want something, I should pay for it!* I do know the difference between right and wrong. I remember the gas and power were shut off, and after the riots, the highway patrol came with shot-guns to turn the power back on. Every day after the first day of the riots, you saw old furniture lined up on the sidewalks on every street. At that time, I had a shotgun, a Mossberg, and stayed at home with it to make sure no one was trying to harm my girlfriend and my baby.

Late news, Koko wants to join me for dinner tomorrow. I will just have one question to ask her. Is there any real reason we have not had sex? I really hope we can make this friendship more than just friendship. So today I asked her. As we went to the Alley, a shopping center, downtown, we found a purse handbag for five bucks. I asked Koko if she was gay, and she said no! But she was not ready for a relationship with sex. Now, I can respect that. Even if it's not what I want. Looks like the pope went to Egypt to the home of the Egyptian pyramids, but he was afraid to visit them in the land of blacks. The pope and I have the same birthday, so he is a real man filled with kindness and care in his heart. And the devil is in the details.

The strike of the writers was called off! Cans of confetti are popping in Hollywood today. Today at the gym training, I saw a ghost like my horoscope had envisioned. It was my friend, Brother Hilton. We used to work the red-carpet events in West Hollywood, Westwood, and Hollywood, with SEM back in the day.

He helped me when some jerk almost provoked me to fight. Right then, I realized that if I were to fight to defend my person, I can't hurt anyone, because I may go to jail. This is a fact which the brother told me about himself. All for some punk-ass job, there is not enough money to pay for pain and suffering of going to jail and not knowing when you be released.

So my goal is to master my emotions and try not to become so emotional when shit doesn't go your way. You know that we don't get all fucked off and act like all the other nut jobs out there. Then every-one will say all kinds of shit because you didn't think through clearly. You really can't trust a female. At least a wise king would not trust a queen with all his heart because one day they can love you and the next day want to cut your balls off as she may be a spy or undercover police. She is a very strange woman, not that all her girlfriends are gold diggers. So deep inside on Sunday, they prayed for forgiveness for the sins that they took against their brother, a.k.a. you, brother. Yet on second thought, she did help you when you could not help yourself. She got you water and food and helped you up the stairs.

So you always remember her good deeds and look over her selfish ways or side. You know now that you may never have sex with her. She will always be a friend, and I would never harm or hurt her in any way, ever! I still can show her I love her and go on with my life. After a certain age in life, you know younger people will take advantage, just because they can. You acted the same way with Uncle Charlie when he was here. Now you know how he was feeling getting old and dying. So sad!

On a positive note, I was working at the shop, and someone's car needed a jump by my car. I went to jump the car, and it started after a few minutes. The battery was almost totally drained. Anyway, the man and woman were about twenty-five and were from South America. The woman picked up my *Hollywood Reporter*, and I say she can have it. The main point is she is an actor shooting a movie, and she said she had a role for me, and it was not paying a lot of money. Cool! I told them to return to the shop for a voltage test. I determined the system was not recharging, so I know how to solve this problem. The mind check is now my dead girlfriend is gone, and I'm not dealing with someone I had sex with for years.

She was not educated. She was wild. She was a party girl with a lot of problems, but you didn't care because she was young and attractive. This other woman is smart, educated, and you can't trust her having a real deep love with you. Even your own mother gave you the heads-up with women. One thing about your mother, she won't give any bad advice most of the time. She is the only one in the world who keeps it real. Sometimes too real. She wiped your nose and your butt with the same towel. Funny, but you know it's true.

Mother's Day 2017

Mom was totally bummed out on Mom's Day. She was all dressed up and ready to go out and have dinner with my sister, who just landed Friday night. She has problems with her innermost parts; she messed on herself. She was upset, and I love you, Mom. I have friends who wish their mother was alive to have any problems with, just to have them back in their lives again no matter what. It will be okay! I'm sending you the *Kong* movie, the new one, and I'm not your Negro.

I was told today by my brother that I can only bring one person to the wedding at the end of the month. I will most likely go alone. Which is okay with me! It will be good to leave the city of stars and look at the real stars a mile higher than you are right now at sea level. And yes, I'm blessed to have my mother still living. And it also reminds me of my grandmother, who has been gone since the seventies. I still remember her and how strange life was back then. My grandmother always treated us with a heavy hand. She was raised in a convent in New Orleans, so now I understand how protective she was of things. As a boy, you may break things because you are so young. I'll never forget, my brother and I were playing in the backyard with the dog named Nicky, who lived in his doghouse in the back. We were throwing rocks or something, which we should not been doing. She called our names, and the next moment, she was pulling us by our ears from the backyard to the front. That was a painful lesson to respect older people. In those days, kids were seen but rarely heard. Any back talk resulted with your ass whipped. The kids today can call the police on their parents. Grandmother gave us tough love. Man might not have landed on the moon, yet they wondered if it was really possible.

My sister just send me a picture of her and my mother and my sister Romel. All smiles and all dressed up! Life is great, and she shows up. I feel bad having not called my ex-wife or Ricky's mother in years. Sharon is not close to Jamal or the rest of the family. Her mother likes me the last time I spoke to her. One wonders what life would have been like if I had stayed married. Does she ever think about me? You can't change or live in the past! I must be okay with the fact that I may never find my mate. Regardless, I must try to seek to be happy, with or without a queen!

Good news: the movie I was in, *The Last Known Escape Artists*, will be at Cannes Film Festival! Hey, there are no small parts, only small actors. It just opened in New York in March. My role is a policeman who slams the lead actor into the patrol car and say it that one line, "Tell it to the judge." City of Stars, are you shining just for me? Someone might see my name on the credits? Yeah right! What the hell have you been smoking? Don't answer that question! Now, the DVD may come out later so the masses can view my work, as short as it may be!

Devil's advocate: a person who opposes an argument with which he does not necessarily disagree as to determine its validity. This is where my head is at! All this desire for fame or something that will not last. It's hard to detach from popular culture. You have got to try "earth." Sometimes I think you might like it!

Today, I saw Mr. Nelson Pickford, a.k.a. Captain. We called him at the park. He wrote for Barry White, "Ecstasy When You Lay Down Next to Me." Yeah, he also sang on the *Rocky* movie soundtrack. I still can't get over the fact that a movie I was in will be in France's biggest stage for movies. An actor's dream-on scale. Superb. In America and Hollywood, I have to face so much discrimination and BS. The world stage of France is a lot bigger setting for the eyes to see in full view. It's been hard to have an international mind in Hollywood. The world sees the small minds here in the USA, and now an open has opened for me, *actor*.

The Man Who has No Imagination Has No Wings (Muhammad Ali)

So my goal is to master my emotions and try not to become so emotional when shit doesn't go your way. You know that we don't get all fucked off and act like all the nut jobs out there. Then everyone will say all kinds of shit because you did not think through clearly. You really can't trust a female. At least a wise king would not trust a queen with all his heart because one day they can love you and the next day want to cut your balls off as she may be a spy or undercover police. She is a very strange woman. She and all her girlfriends are gold diggers. So deep inside on Sunday, they prayed for forgiveness for the sins against their brother, a.k.a. you, brother.

Yet on second thought, she did help you when you could not help yourself. She got your water and food and helped you up the stairs. So you must remember her good deeds and overlook her shortcoming. She's only human. You know now you may never have sex with her. She will always be a friend, and I would never harm or hurt her in anyway, ever!

I still can show her I love her and go on with my life. You know, younger people will take advantage just because they can. You acted the same way; now the shoe is on the other foot.

Once again, there was the desire to go out and have sex with some loser bitches and all those sluts fucking other sluts. I have got to let these negative feeling out. One of the reasons for this book is self-expression. It's hard to be a human being, a black man, and an actor (with the sound of fireworks in the back ground). Still, I'm happy for many things. Peace of mind is always a start to a positive mental thinking! It's very hard to master one's thoughts! Fuck the world and all its problems. I can't help it. I did not choose my color; I'm not subhuman. They don't know me but judge me. That's not smart at all! You can lead a horse to water, but you make slower peaceful vibe. My body is relaxed after a hard work out; now I can focus on my mind. Relaxing that mindfulness is very hard to control. To really quiet my mind, reset the soul. At this point in my life, I can take this path. (Rap music blasting next door. More fireworks firing in the distance.) Living in a black hood, you never know what to expect.

By God, if I had never been to England and other places in the world, I don't know what man I would have become in this urban mind-set. This book will be one of a kind. *Marine Vision* will turn a lot of heads. I know there are funny facts but serious subjects as well! Food for thought (police cars full of noise in the distance), I do feel better writing stuff down. (Car horns sounding off. One louder horn sound, and now airplane engine fly overhead.) I can hear a lot of car movements outside. For real, my so-called love life is in La La Land, not based on real facts. You have been played. Shit! I worked hard for the ring that you don't ever wear. Pressure: The cards are stacked against you. Most people say yes! Should you end this relationship before her birthday, that way you can pick up a little of your pride? The ego burn will heal in time. I hope! My uncle Richard did not believe in God, and I admit it has been a while since I read the Quran and prayed five times a day. The hands of God are like fingers pointing to the sky. Each path is all part of God. He has blessed me to live this long, and my mother is alive. And yes, God may be a *she*. Some of us can reason things out!

Play the devil's advocate. You don't want to ever lose her friendship just yet, not now, and next month is baby's birthday, and she would have been forty. Never been married, never wanted to be. She had three kids and was never close to any of them, but she was the close friend and female. No one can ever fill the void, the darkness of losing someone you cared so much about. I can't change the past, nor should I want to change it! The man who has no imagination has no wings. If Ali were alive today, he would see many sad things. The world is in a dark place right now. There is sad news from England, which I consider to be my home away from home. 007 passed away today. To add to sadness is the fact that I may have broken up with Koko. I'm in real tears and sad feeling.

But we all must carry on, no need time to heal. The hurt is deep and strong, heart-breaking, down to the very core. We will get past it somehow. Hell, you father just lost a leg, and you are crying over a woman. He might consider that weakness. Wimps need not apply.

This is pressure and pain on a new level!

The real thing is the words and expressions have no sense. Questions come to mind. Is there anything I can do to feel better about human relationships? Pressure and pain on a new level. Can we control the dark places in our minds? We are all family. Look at the mess people have made with their lives. People are talking about me because I hear my ears ringing. God helps the folks in the UK. England gave me some of the best experiences as a lad. It opened my mind to a different world. It is the land of the greatest writer who ever lived. Land where the first rules of law were signed by the king. It is where I was lucky to have an English teacher to teach me about grammar, world history, math, science, art, how to serve tea, and how to save rainwater in barrels for washing your face. I remember seeing African kings in the London Museum. I learned how to ride my first motorbike and fell in love with the MGB sports car. But when bad things happen, no one really ever knows the root problem, but who really cares? The pain does not give up. Everything seems upside down. I can feel it! Been there many times, then you understand in time things will never be the same from that point on. Something is turned off, PTSD in full force. Many a Marine know what that's like first-hand. And some never recover, but now on a mass level for everyone, don't stop the pain.

Hard Times on Planet Earth

With all the horror in the world, mindless acts, the world is on fire. Pain and depression are everywhere in the world. It's hard to find kindness in the world. One must be mindful when with others. I must plan for my trip for the wedding next week. I can make this trip more relaxed now after having sex, hot and nasty sex. Hollywood Marine putting in work—that definitely takes my mind off Koko and takes pressure out my life for a few hours. Just what a man needs. I am sorry, Buddha. It's hard for me now to want to fuck with a female even at my age. The world is so much in deep depression. Panic, pain, and fear are all around. This is how the world is being ruled. There is always going to be a war of good versus evil. Brother Chuck Norris would say that the good guys wear black, but not the good guys are black? For now, I am going to do the work; my teacher expects me to go on with life and carry on training and work hard for my body and mind. All this and to live to see another day.

Being an actor and a black man in America is hard as hell! I'm so tired of all this war stuff. I will always love home, the USA, but there are devils out there making this hell for everyone! That really sucks! What are we teaching our kids? They think this is how humans must act because of all they see. People are just hurt and mad; it is very hard to find peace. My training is going well; I do see improvement in my body. I'm not taking any weed with me on the trip. It's not worth the bullshit! I'm black going to an all-white dry state. Don't slip. I don't need any problems. I'm glad my grandchild talked to my mother this week. Cheer the old girl up and make a bond. Life is good! Sex takes off the pressure; it is much needed. My mind is more relaxed. Koko was stressing me out! I should blame her. It is more the world than her. She is a good actor, a very smart woman, problems with simple communication. We are all getting older. She is also, starting to fade in appeal. I have to see the full circle of events;

that is why I'm writing to tell my story. They kill the people you love, kids. How heartless man can be! It's hard to pray to a god who would allow bad things to the smallest weakest person. Koko just made you realize how the odds are really against you because of your age and skin color in Hollywood. But shoo that! I learned my act in England. I can look back at the good times in the movie industry. They can never overpay a veteran for his or her service. I must plan for this trip.

Now the adventure is written, a solo ride for miles end, seeing miles and miles of Utah, racing to the Colorado River to the mountain high in the sky. Blood-red rocks high as any sky-high building. The strawberry moon is in the sky today. What that means, who knows? The trail to Denver is a long hard road. I was taking a big risk that my car may or may not make it all the way like the Marine Corps drill strike up the hill, down the hill, around the hill! We went all the way with a few unseen problems, but thanks to the cosmos for helping me find my way back safely. It was a big step, but it worked out okay! Many people would not take on a solo trip. I thank the Most High I don't think like everyone else. If I had to take someone, it may have been more problems with bathroom limits and food breaks, and rooms once I got to where I was going. Driving eighty miles for hours was a toil on the mind and body, but the light inside of me was flying high with excitement on every turn and corner, following miles and miles of river from the great mountains that lead a mile in the sky! No time for the weak at heart.

I have not a clue of what I would have done if the car had broken down. The fact is that the car is sound and worked hard to the dry smoking heat across the salt flats of Utah and the hot sands of two more states. This makes me glad I live at sea level, with Marine clouds in the morning prayer filling the body with ease!

June 3, 2017, Saturday

Today, Brother Muhammad Ali has been gone now for a year. We all miss him, and by we, I mean the whole wide world. The wedding is sometime today. The event is high in the mountains, evergreen trees everywhere, forest with rivers that go everywhere. I can truly say I've been to the mountaintop, like Brother King would say. Wedding music flew at the evergreens. A boy and girl threw flowers in the wind while the vows where exchanged, a day every woman dreams of, I guess. What the hell do I know what women's dream about? Meanwhile, in the real whole world, a woman dies in a rafting accident on the Upper Colorado River, and I almost hit a deer that had been killed by some other car or truck on the way home near Love Land. I thought about my dear Bambi, who was killed on a dark highway in the city. The Black Hawk Casino stage, a mile in the sky, is the place where Arrowhead water is drawn clear clean water. Aspen and Vail and Loveland. The mountains are so high up they affect your air intake because the air is so thin. You must drink water to take the pressure off your ears. The long ride was going beyond the beyond, stopping in Vegas to place a ten-spot on a playoff game at the Gold Nuggets. Even driving at night to miles and miles of canyons, bright red, from Arizona to you gets about three hundred miles. You can see the Rocky Mountains about the mountaintops. One has to remember that the Rocky Mountains are an hour ahead of us in the west. Going there, you lose an hour, and on the way back, you gain an hour. Strange how that works. A solo adventure about nine hundred miles uphill. Climate goes from superhot to mountain showers. When one finds out the truth, it is more difficult than one might think! A question I have myself all these months have come to an end. As you get older in life, there are certain things you must realize as time goes on. Peace has to come from within, not from without. A quote from Buddha speaks so much in simple words that anyone could understand. This trip really opened up my mind to see a great area of the work in the salt flats rock solid formations higher and bigger that most skylines.

You can see waterlines in the rock that may have been floods hundreds of years ago. What was queer was that I was at one place where I was in a small town, and everyone was asleep on Sunday and everything in the town was close, even the police department. There was no one to ask directions, not even with the sun up. The gas card did not read. Okay, I am ready to freak out. I am thinking, I am in the middle of nowhere with no money. The problem was solved when I pulled up money at an ATM. The gas station opens at the time.

June 11, 2017, Sunday

Bambi's birthday is this week. Rest in peace. I wish she were alive, even if she was on drugs, but the fact remains the same.

She was a good lover and a good friend. She knew me more than anyone at that time. She was wild and sweet and funny and carefree. She never was fake! Ghetto love ain't about crap. Now the problem is, What am I going to do with a son who has no basic skills and not willing or is not able to get his life on track? He keeps making the same mistakes with the cars he buys that are junk. His world would be better if he had the basics down. "The man who has no imagination has no wings." A quote from Brother Muhammad Ali.

She tried to act like a mother for Ricky. Back in the day, she would walk him to school, and I know she loved him. She got drunk one night, and went to the house of Ricky's foster folks and asked to see Ricky. It was sad, but it was funny as I look back. I gave two people my business cards in Las Vegas with a picture of Ali and myself. I know he was a fan because he worn an Ali T-shirt. That makes his day. That and the winning ticket on the baseball playoffs. Mine was $30.

All Is Paradox

"The movement of the Great Integrity is infinite, yet its character is passive. Being defines every form of life, yet all originate in, and return to, non-being" (Tao Te Ching).

The solid rock formations are painted in my mind. This formation runs for hundreds of miles. It has been here since the dawn of time. One starts to realize how small we are to the grand design. One of the good things about driving is not the fact that you are alone, but not using the phone or smart junk to keep you hyper than hype. Even the TV you see is different, right-wing TV, in Denver. White males for drugs, guns, and the like. The phone is useless in some parts of some states, so you are screwed if you need it; event could happen high in the mountains also. Thank goodness, I have been to the mountaintop and seen its wonders that I could never get by air. If I had seen a UFO in Vegas, that would have been superb. The fact is I took a chance, and it paid off. As I return to a place called Hollywood with millions of folks, it feels different now, because I understand that there is only one me in this time and space. I hope this book will help young men realized that it's a big world out there and you are part of it all while you are here. Rivers of love is what it's not! Be wise as you can, learn as much as you can.

About the Author

Asmar Muhammad loves working on cars and acting in films, plays, and TV. He used to ride motorcycles and walk on the beach. James Bond films, Bruce Lee films, and Jim Kelly films.

Education: Highland Grade School (Vallejo, California), London Central High School (London, England), Highlands High School (North Highlands, California), Highline Community College (Midway, Washington), the Evergreen State College (Olympia, Washington), political science, media, National Technical Schools (Los Angeles). He earned an associate in science in automotive diagnostics.

Awards: United States Marine Corps Awards, Pastry Baking Award, Traffic Safety Education Award, Outstanding Volunteer Services, Hollywood Recreation Center, Los Angeles City, associate of arts in professional acting in Merrick Studios of Dramatic Arts, Hollywood, California.

This book is inspired by Sister Souljah, Lola St. Vil, Brandy Leeann Thompson, Marilyn Burruss, Mariah Brown.

CPSIA information can be obtained
at www.ICGtesting.com
Printed in the USA
BVHW07s2229280518
517560BV00003B/382/P

9 781642 142501